NORTH YORKSHIRE POLICE

RITUAL CRIME UNIT
(NORTH)

OFFICIAL PURPOSES ONLY

The enclosed document has been assessed and
classified as <u>SENSITIVE MATERIAL</u>

Investigating Officer's Signature:

Erlichardu

DOCUMENT NUMBER: 10 / 150

If you believe you have witnessed a magical crime,
report it anonymously via Twitter to @abaddonbooks

An Abaddon Books™ Publication
www.abaddonbooks.com
abaddon@rebellion.co.uk

First published in 2013 by Abaddon Books™, Rebellion Intellectual
Property Limited, Riverside House, Osney Mead, Oxford, OX2 0ES, UK.

10 9 8 7 6 5 4 3 2 1

Editor-in-Chief: Jonathan Oliver
Commissioning Editor: David Moore
Cover & Design: Sam Gretton
Marketing and PR: Michael Molcher
Publishing Manager: Ben Smith
Creative Director and CEO: Jason Kingsley
Chief Technical Officer: Chris Kingsley

ISBN: 978-1-78108-257-7

RITUAL CRIME UNIT

UNDER THE SKIN

F. E. RICHARDSON

ABADDON
BOOKS

In memory of Lesley Richardson,
my mother and my biggest fan.

CHAPTER ONE

THE POLICE VAN jolted over the potholes of the rough farm roads at speed. DCI Claire Pierce gripped her paper cup tighter before the coffee could spill over and slop down the front of her tac vest.

Might have been the best place for it. "Christ, what the hell am I drinking? Did you run it through a goat before you gave it to me?" She chugged down the rest of the coffee without waiting for an answer. Any method of caffeine delivery was better than none.

Sergeant Mistry gave her a brief grin from the other side of the van. "Not my fault, Guv," he said. "North Yorkshire Police supplied the coffee."

"Yeah? Well, next time we call for a raid remind me to pencil it in on the budget." Pierce grimaced as she reached the bottom of the cup. It was all right for Deepan. He was barely closing in on thirty, still looking only half that with his chubby cheeks and artfully gelled hair. At fifty-four, she was considerably less bright and breezy. She wasn't keen to be out as late as this, but they didn't have much choice. The full moon was their best opportunity to catch the skinbinder they were after in the act.

There had to be one operating illegally in the area. They'd been chasing reports of unlicensed shapeshifters across Yorkshire for six months. This many enchanted pelts couldn't all be heirloom pieces dragged down from the attic, and the maker's rune on the one bearskin they'd seized didn't belong to any of the country's six authorised skin shops. Weeks of painstaking police work had finally led the Ritual Crime Unit to a farmhouse that the neighbours claimed had seen exotic animals delivered.

Pierce gripped the side wall of the van as the young driver swung them off the main road and through the farm gate. She didn't know his name. This team was only half hers, the numbers made up by North Yorkshire Police. Necessary with the RCU's limited manpower, but still not a happy thought. If there were shapeshifters on site, a group of untrained uniforms in hi-visibility vests were about as much use to contain them as a strip of Police Do Not Cross tape.

She could see the dark shape of the farmhouse coming up on their left, the stones lit by the headlights of the Armed Response Vehicle ahead. Beyond was a brick-built barn with a white van parked outside. The owners of the property were supposed to be in Spain.

Pierce reached for the radio on her vest.

"Leo. Your people ready?"

"*Just give us the word.*" The familiar gruff voice was cool and steady. Leo Grey she'd worked with before, the local Firearms Support Unit's specialist in supernatural threats. At least he'd be packing silver bullets in his Glock, but the ammo was rare and expensive, and the rest of his team were only supplied with Tasers. Theory said they should work just fine on shifters.

Pierce wasn't a great fan of trusting to theory.

"I want you with me in the barn," she said. "If the skinbinder's at work, that's where he'll be." Skinning was a messy business. The animals had to be freshly slaughtered for the skinbinding ritual to be performed.

"*I hear you. Henderson, you're with us,*" he told one of his team. "*Baker will lead the rest of the team on the house clearance.*"

Dividing their forces made her edgy, but with a site this big they couldn't afford to risk their suspects escaping in the dark. "Constable Keane and I will be coming in behind you." Pierce exchanged a glance of acknowledgement with Sally Keane, the RCU's resident expert in shapeshifting pelts. A plump, easy-going woman with blonde hair and red-framed glasses, she looked out of place stuffed into a tac vest, but Pierce knew she could handle herself in a crisis. It wasn't her own people that concerned her.

As she climbed out of the van, Pierce checked her belt for her silver cuffs and incapacitant spray. Limited use against a shifter that wasn't already subdued, but that was why they had Firearms along.

"All right, you know your orders," she said as the team assembled on the grass. "No heroics. You see a shifter coming at you, you get out of the way and call for Firearms Support." She looked over at Leo, and he gave her a terse nod. "Okay, everybody get into position. We're going in."

Leo took the lead as they advanced on the old barn at a jog. He must have been past forty, but he kept himself in shape, a lean, craggy-faced man with the kind of sandy blond hair that didn't show the grey. As she followed him across the grass, Pierce tried to tug her own ill-fitting tac vest into a more comfortable position, vowing yet again to give up living on microwave meals. Slim chance of that.

Her stomach tensed as Leo and Henderson adopted positions to either side of the barn's wooden door. Leo had his Glock held out before him in a two-handed grip, the barrel pointed down at the grass between them. Henderson had his hand on his Taser. They exchanged sober nods.

Henderson threw the door open and Leo charged in ahead of him. "Police! Get down on the ground!" he shouted. "Everybody stop what you're doing and get down on the ground!" Pierce followed right on their heels, Sally and a swarm of North Yorkshire's finest close behind her.

The barn was unconverted, a high-roofed open space with wooden beams and a dirt floor. Crates and vaguer shapes covered by tarpaulins were shoved against the walls to clear the centre. A square window in the rear wall allowed the full moon's light to spill inside. The pool of moonlight and the glow of their police torches lit up a gruesome scene. The bloody corpse of a grey wolf was strung up, dangling from a beam, the half-skinned pelt peeled down over the muscle like a fur glove pulled inside out. The dead-eyed face reminded Pierce of her neighbour's pet husky.

No time to get sentimental. They'd caught the skinbinder in the act.

Focused on his craft, the young man didn't even turn, swaying and crooning to himself as he moved around the hanging carcass. In the shadows he looked hunched, misshapen, until she realised that bound to his back were a great set of eagle's wings, incongruous against a dark T-shirt and frayed jeans. His bare arms were covered with tattooed runes, and in one hand he held a curved silver knife with a hooked end.

"Drop the knife!" Leo demanded, moving closer but not yet ready to raise the pistol. Henderson followed a few paces behind, pivoting to look into the shadows as he passed. Sally moved after him and bent to lift one of the tarpaulins, pulling her torch from the clip on her vest and peering underneath.

Pierce kept her eyes on the skinbinder, not willing to trust he was as absorbed as he seemed. He was still humming, maintaining his focus as he made ritual incisions in the carcass. She was damn glad Leo and his people were professionals, not trigger-happy hotheads looking for a chance to fire. This could still end without tears, if they were careful.

"Holy *shit*." The curse from Sally drew her eyes away from the standoff. Pierce saw the young constable drop the raised tarp and jerk back. "Guv, we've got skins here," she said, swallowing as she looked up. "But I think they're—"

In the moment of distraction, the skinbinder made his move.

A flash of silver motion at the corner of her eye. Pierce spun just in time to see Henderson reel backwards, clutching his arm where the skinning knife had gashed it.

"Drop the knife!" Leo shouted again, raising his gun, but before he could fire a dark shape dropped from the roof beams, slamming into him and sending him staggering into the hanging carcass. As the thing bounded forward, launching from his shoulders, Pierce glimpsed gold feline eyes and a flash of yellow fangs.

A black panther.

Not a real one. "Shapeshifter!" she bellowed.

"Fuck!" Henderson scrambled backward, fumbling for the Taser at his side, but it was a clumsy move, reaching across himself with his uninjured arm. Before he could draw the weapon, the shapeshifter was on him, its jaws crunching down on his shoulder. It shook him like a toy and tossed him aside to slam against the wall. Pierce heard the crack of breaking bone.

"Officer down!" she shouted into her radio. "We need backup in the barn! Shapeshifter in the building!" Leo shoved the swinging wolf carcass aside to get a clear shot, but with everyone's torches moving at once the barn was a blur of shifting shadows.

"I've got Henderson, Guv!" Sally said, darting across the barn toward the injured man. But the shifter spun about as fast as any real cat, claws flashing out to rake across her throat. Her cry of shock strangled into a gurgle as she staggered back, a spray of blood spattering the dirt floor.

"Shit!" Pierce saw the shifter's head swinging towards her, and she grabbed for her spray. Wouldn't stop the damn thing, but it might drive it out, save the casualties from any further harm...

The deafening blast of a close-quarters gunshot echoed in her ears. It plunged her into instant ringing, muffled deafness, like the world heard from the bottom of a pool. Even that didn't soften the retort of the next shot.

The big cat jerked back as the bullet ripped into its shoulder—and, like an optical illusion, it was no longer a panther, but a man crouched on all fours with the pelt draped across his back. Taking no chances, Pierce lunged forward and slapped her silver cuffs on his tattooed arms, yanking his wrists together with no time to be careful of his shoulder. The man snapped his teeth towards her, still half lost in the mind of the beast.

But neutralised for now. If the silver bullet hadn't ruined the magic of the pelt, the cuffs would definitely stop him using it. Pierce straightened up—and spotted the skinbinder she'd half forgotten running towards the back of the barn. "Freeze!" she yelled, her own voice dulled in her ears to the point where she could hardly tell how loud she was shouting. "There's no way out!"

The skinbinder ignored her and took a running leap towards the window. It was an impossible jump... but as he left the ground, his body collapsed in on itself, bones folding away at impossible angles like a closing umbrella. The heavy wings on his back moulded into his outflung arms; his bent legs sunk inwards and curved into talons; his moonlit face elongated, stretching out into a hooked beak.

The great shape of the eagle soared away out of the window, disappearing into the dark night. Leo swore and ran forward to aim after it, but too late to take the shot.

"Eagle shifter coming out of the back of the barn!" Pierce shouted it into her radio, but she knew that no one outside would have a chance to stop him.

She turned to move towards the injured officers. It was clear that neither one would be getting up without help. Didn't look much like they would get up at all.

Jesus Christ. What a clusterfuck.

CHAPTER TWO

IT TOOK LONGER than Pierce liked to get the injured off the scene and the prisoner on his way to the station. She sent Deepan back to accompany him; she didn't trust jittery uniforms with a shapeshifter. The bullet should have rendered the pelt's enchantment inert, but that was still no reason to take chances. The panther's wound hadn't transferred to the man; small injuries were repaired in the flux of shifting bodies. It took major organ damage to kill a shapeshifter in animal form.

Police officers weren't so lucky.

Pierce would have liked to send one of their own off in the ambulance with Sally, but they were stretched far too thin as it was with a crime scene this size. In a perfect world, she'd have had two prisoners in custody right now, and Sally here to check the barn over for magical traps. Instead they had a loose skinbinder to watch out for, and she was stuck here waiting for Tim Cable to show up.

Tim wouldn't have been her first choice to bring on a bust like this. Three months in the Unit and still earnest as a puppy, he was textbook perfect on all the procedures—which might do him some good if they ever actually drew a textbook case. The books weren't even written to cover RCU work; when Pierce had first joined up, the only reference to consult was George, the cranky old sergeant who'd been around longer than God's mother-in-law. What she hadn't learned from him, she'd picked up through trial-and-error, and things that hadn't killed her yet.

Tonight was a grim reminder there could always be a first time.

She chewed the lip of another cardboard cup of coffee as the forensics van pulled up. The crime scene photographer who got out was half familiar, a weary-looking blonde woman with her tripod in hand. "Why is it you lot from Ritual always call us out to scenes in the middle of the night and the middle of nowhere?" she asked.

"Ritual magic. Brings out your average criminal's flair for amateur dramatics." Pierce turned her torch toward the open barn door. "Through there."

The photographer assessed the scene with a practised eye. "Just the barn?"

Slim chance they'd get much of value from the rest of the scene, with the number of feet that had been trampling over it. "Just the barn," she echoed with a curt nod. "Bloodstains on the left and most of the footprints are from the attack on our people. We need pictures of the rear window and the rafters— one of our suspects went out the back, and the other one came from above. Make sure you get that knife there on the ground."

The skinbinder had dropped the ritual blade in his escape— the silver would have stopped him from transforming. With any luck, they'd be able to lift some prints from it. In the shadowy dark of the barn she hadn't seen if he wore gloves, but she doubted he'd have risked it. Complex magic took precision, and the smallest bit of clumsiness could compromise a ritual.

"The dead wolf is relevant too, I'm guessing?" the photographer said. She wrinkled her mouth at the gruesome sight. "Poor puppy." She snapped off a few establishing shots.

"Guv?"

Pierce turned to see Tim hurrying towards her from the collection of cars. A lanky boy with short spiked hair and glasses, he wasn't quite as young and gormless as he looked, but sometimes it was easy to forget that.

"Sally was injured?" he asked, his eyes wide.

"They've taken her to hospital. You can call them for news later, but right now I need you to assess the scene. We need to know there are no magical surprises around the place before forensics start disturbing things." Self-destructing evidence was her least favourite kind.

Tim nodded solemnly. "Right, Guv." But he hovered for a moment, clearly at a loss for where to start. "Um... I should... check outside the thresholds for trigger runes?" He looked to her for approval, still caught up in the habit of treating every case like an assessment.

She'd have to shake that out of him before she sent him off on his own to butt heads with local forces who thought rank outweighed specialist expertise. She flicked a hand to send him off to do as he thought best.

A cultured voice interrupted from behind them. "That won't be necessary, thank you, Constable."

Apparently being a DCI didn't spare her from butting heads either. Pierce turned to face the new arrival.

He was a tall man in his late thirties, with thick dark hair and the kind of blandly handsome looks that were a nightmare of anyone trying to take down a useful description. He wore a black cashmere coat, the shirt collar and dark tie beneath as crisp as if he'd come straight from the ironing board.

Never trust a police detective who didn't look like he lived in his clothes. Assuming this man *was* with the police; if he wasn't and he'd still got through the cordon, heads would be rolling very soon. Pierce fixed him with a hard stare. "Sorry, you would be?"

He strode forward to meet her, unsmiling. "Jason Maitland, Counter Terror Action Team." That was a new one on her, but then they changed the names on these things more often than she changed her sheets, and the ID that he flashed at her looked real enough. "I'm afraid my people are going to need to take over this site."

And if that didn't smell rancid, she didn't know what did. She narrowed her eyes. "There's no reason for Counter Terrorism to take an interest in this case." A rogue skinbinder was a threat on several levels, but none of them involved national security.

"We have our reasons. I'm afraid I can't discuss them." Stock phrases, no apology behind them.

Dark suited figures were already moving across the site, herding the uniformed officers away. They even had their own forensics people, pouring out of an unmarked black van in coveralls. Terrorism was a buzzword with plenty of political clout—but Pierce had her own field of authority.

"This is an RCU case," she said, standing firm. "We can't allow anyone to start handling the evidence until it's been cleared as safe by our experts."

By her side she sensed Tim shifting, uncomfortable at being caught in a power struggle, but she wasn't about to concede ground by breaking eye contact with Maitland.

If he was ruffled by the challenge, he didn't show it. "We have our own specialists in ritual magic," he said.

"Specialists? From where?" She raised a sceptical eyebrow. True experts were thin on the ground, and ones with police training even more so. She could count the members of the RCU's northern branch without resorting to toes, and its southern counterpart wasn't much bigger. Either Maitland was overestimating the knowledge of his specialists, or someone was playing silly buggers with the allocation of police resources. The RCU was struggling to put together a useful crime database as it was without some shadowy subdepartment out there duplicating their efforts.

"All fully PRMC certified," Maitland said. The same qualification the Unit required—and stuck with a wet-behind-the-ears rookie as she was right now, Pierce couldn't even claim to have greater field experience on her side. She stepped back out of his way with a scowl.

"Two good officers were injured making this bust," she reminded him. "This suspect has been top of the RCU's most wanted list for months."

"I assure you, we're not going to let him go free." Maitland's flash of teeth was more predatory than reassuring. "He's been top of *our* most wanted list for even longer."

"But you can't tell me why."

His smile broadened into an even less likeable expression. "I'm sure you understand the realities of these things." He straightened up, already dismissing her from his attention. "Now, if you could please have your people clear the scene as fast as possible. The longer we delay here, the greater our suspect's lead on us becomes."

Our suspect. Her lips curved in bitter acknowledgement. They weren't going to win any concessions here. "Of course," she said, and held his gaze for a few seconds longer before turning to stalk away across the long grass. "Come on, Tim. Let's go."

The young constable chased after her like a bewildered puppy. "Are we just leaving, then?" he said, looking back over his shoulder.

"I'm going back to the station," she said. "He might have taken over our crime scene, but we've still got a prisoner to interview."

SHE GOT TIM to drive her back to the station. The journey passed mostly in silence, barring the lingering tinnitus from the gunshots. The headache only shortened her temper as she stewed in her own irritation.

There'd been no hint of a terrorist connection to the case before this. They still hadn't uncovered the skinbinder's identity—so what the hell did Maitland and his team know that they didn't? If Counter Terrorism had been watching the farm for reasons of their own, they should have been coordinating with the local police so both sides knew before the raid went down. The way things had shaken out, it felt uncomfortably like her team had been used to do someone else's dirty work, then kicked out.

"Do you need me here, Guv?" Tim asked as he stopped the car outside the station.

Pierce flapped a hand at him. "No. Go home." Somebody was going to need to be fresh tomorrow morning, and it clearly wasn't going to be her. She snagged another no doubt ill-advised cup of coffee before heading down to the cells.

Arthur Jakes, the Custody Sergeant, was there to let her in through the barred gate. A stout, broad-faced man with salt-and-pepper hair leaning towards the salt side, he'd been part of the scenery here for as long as she'd been at the station.

"Did Deepan bring our shifter in?" she asked him as the gate clanged shut behind her.

Jakes nodded. "Yep. We had a fun time with that one. Took a bite out of Constable Carter while they were stripping him out of his skin."

"Did you get a name?" She wasn't optimistic.

"Ha, yes. One Mr 'Grrr.'"

She gave that a wry smile that she doubted it deserved. "Did you put him in the special cell?"

With the RCU's limited budget, they only had one cell built to handle supernatural strength. A shifter removed from his pelt should be no more danger than a normal human, but Pierce wasn't prepared to bet the farm on it. Those who wore their animal forms too long or too often didn't always turn all the way back. Ritual magic was never as safe and controlled as its practitioners might like to believe.

"We did, but he's in interview right now," he said. Pierce turned to stare at him.

"Deepan took him in for questioning without me?" She would have thought he'd have realised she'd want to be in on this one.

Jakes shook his head. "No, these weren't your lot. Counter Terror Action Men, or some such bollocks. Had the proper authorisation so I let them in." He peered over his glasses at her scowl. "Problem?"

Pierce grimaced, but shook her head. "Mine, not yours," she said. If Maitland's people had authorisation from Superintendent Palmer, there was nothing she or Jakes could do about it. "They were throwing their weight around at the crime scene, too. Waited for us to make the bust, then kicked us all out as soon as the fur had stopped flying."

"I did hear it flew." Jakes pursed his lips in sympathy. "How's Sally?"

"Still no word," she said, and gave a tired sigh. If she'd known they were going to be turfed off the crime scene without the chance to collect evidence, she would have sent someone along in the ambulance.

She stared at the wall of the interview room, wishing she had a good excuse to storm in and take over. Tempting though it might be, squabbling in front of the suspect could only harm their chances of getting anything out of him.

She turned to Sergeant Jakes. "Do we have audio on the interview room CCTV?"

He snorted. "And waste his lordship's precious pennies when the interviews are all taped anyway? You jest, my lady. It's video only." He turned one of the charge desk monitors around so she could see it.

Not that it showed anything she couldn't have pictured for herself. The interviewers were both nondescript men in grey suits; the shifter that sat across from them lounged casually in his chair, still something subtly feline about his posture. Not a huge man, but solidly muscular, with a broad jaw and shaved head. The camera angle showed part of an intricate tattoo on his neck, no doubt a match for the corresponding maker's rune inside the panther pelt. She doubted that she'd get a chance to check, with Maitland intent on seizing all her evidence. She scowled.

It was impossible to tell what the interviewers were asking, but the responses came through loud and clear on camera. Studied indifference, the occasional curve of a cynical smirk; no protestations of innocence here, just the relaxed arrogance of a man who either expected to walk free or didn't care that he wouldn't.

She needed to be in there, asking her own questions and watching for the tell-tale twitches that an audio recording wouldn't show. Assuming she would even be allowed to listen to it; the national security umbrella could be used to cover all sorts of things.

"I don't suppose you can lip-read?" she asked the desk sergeant.

"And find out what the prisoners are saying about me?" He raised a hand to his heart. "I prefer to imagine they all think I'm lovely."

"Everyone thinks you're lovely, Arthur," she said absently. A flicker of something on the monitor caught her eye. Just a brief flash of darkness in between the shifter's lips seen as he sneered, maybe no more than a shadow on the footage.

Maybe not. She held up a hand to stop Jakes as he began to speak.

"Did those idiots let Deepan check the suspect over before they took charge?" she asked, her eyes still focused on the screen.

A faint motion in her peripheral vision as the sergeant shook his head. "Insisted on doing it all by themselves. Something up?" He rounded the desk to watch the monitor with her.

"I'm not sure." *Come on, you bastard...* Pierce tried to will the shifter into opening his mouth.

And there it was. A split second glimpse inside his mouth as he made another soundless jeer, and this time she saw it for sure: the shapeshifter's tongue was turning black.

"Shit!" She turned and sprinted for the interview room.

Jakes ran with her without questioning why, the keys jangling at his belt. As she threw the door open the two interviewers jumped up from their seats, and the nearest tried to crowd them back outside. "Chief Inspector! You shouldn't be in here. This interview concerns potentially sensitive information—"

"You idiots," she shouted. "He's got a suicide rune in his mouth! We need to get him to—"

But it was far too late. Sprawling back in his chair, glassy-eyed, the shifter still managed to offer her a mocking grin. His gums were black, the teeth loose in their sockets, and decay wafted out on his panting breaths like halitosis.

"Get medical!" she shouted at Jakes, though there was nothing they could do. The man was rotting from the inside out.

Dark spots began to blossom on his skin, spreading quickly into open sores. His eyeballs blackened and burst like crushed grapes, thick tarry goo oozing down sunken cheeks. By now what skin remained was bruise-black, thin as paper, like fragile fabric stretched over a frame. One of Maitland's men grabbed his arm, trying to pull him up, but the rotting flesh just tore with a wet squelch.

Within seconds, the decaying form was barely even human anymore; just a hollowed, shrivelled, blackened *thing* collapsing in on itself.

Outside in the hallway the alarms wailed, summoning help that was already too late. The shapeshifter was dead—and any secrets that he might have revealed had died with him.

CHAPTER THREE

By the time the medical team arrived, there was little to be done with the prisoner except scrape his oozing remains off the furniture. The stench of decay and death lingered on her clothes and in her throat even after several sprays of deodorant and yet another mug of coffee. She'd given up on getting to bed tonight.

If Pierce was resigned to being stuck at work until the early hours, Superintendent Palmer was bloody furious about it.

"This has been a complete cock-up from start to finish!" he said, hands clasped behind his back as he paced his office. He was a finicky little man, shorter than her and probably a few years younger, though you wouldn't know it from the receding hairline. Under normal circumstances he would have been happy to sleep through their after-dark raid and hear about the results in the morning, but Maitland's interference and the news of a death in police custody had dragged him out of bed and back to work.

And Pierce was the one who got called onto the carpet to account for it. If Maitland's two men were getting a bollocking for their part in this fiasco, it was taking place in private, with no opportunity for her to stick her oar in.

Which was a pity, because she had plenty to say. "Sir, the team from Counter Terrorism came waltzing in throwing their weight about and overrode all our procedures," she said. "My people would have checked the prisoner for ritual markings if they'd only been allowed to do their jobs. We're lucky it was just a suicide rune and not something worse. He *could* have taken half the station down."

"Lucky," he echoed, with a bitter twist to the word. He whirled about to face her. "Yes, Claire, I feel exceptionally *lucky* that the resource-intensive, high-profile raid *you* persuaded me to authorise has resulted in two injured officers, one suspect escaped, and another one dead in our custody!"

Now was not the time to argue. "Sir." She acknowledged the words with a carefully neutral expression, staring past him at the crime statistics posted up on the wall. The RCU lagging behind, as usual.

Palmer spent several more moments pacing himself out before he stopped and heaved a defeated sigh. He fixed her with a cool gaze. "A suicide rune," he said.

"Yes, sir." She nodded. "It would have been tattooed on the inside of his mouth. He only needed to hold his tongue against it for a set length of time to trigger the rune." She'd seen it before, though it had been over a decade ago; some ridiculous apocalypse cult or other with a vow to take their secrets to the grave.

He ran a hand back through his thinning hair. "Then it couldn't have been prevented?"

"It might have, if they'd allowed a team with the proper expertise to take charge," she said. "Sir, I don't know who these people are, or what their interest is in this skinbinder, but there's no way they're half as qualified as the RCU to handle supernatural crime. This should be *our* case."

Palmer pressed his lips together and gave another sigh, pulling the chair out from under his desk to sit down. "That's as may be, but it's not your decision to make—or mine," he said, shaking his head as he leaned back. "This is coming from above my head, Claire. The Counter Terror Action Team have full autonomy to do as they see fit, and we are to give them our cooperation."

"No questions asked, of course." Pierce scowled.

He gave her a stern look. "You understand perfectly well how important information security can be. Loose lips sink ships, and all that."

"On the other hand, maybe if we'd loosened some, we might have found the suicide runes hidden behind them."

He threw up his hands. "I can see that you're not going to drop this, but there's only so far even *you* can get running on stubbornness." He checked the time on his fancy silver watch and gave a grimace. "Go home, get some sleep, and consider this case off your desk and best forgotten. It's the Counter Terror Action Team's problem now."

PIERCE HAD LEARNED to sleep like the dead no matter how grim a day she'd come home from, but that alone didn't make three hours substitute for a night's rest. She dragged herself reluctantly out of bed, skipping the minimal time she had to make breakfast in favour of a phone call to Sally's husband.

He sounded more exhausted than she was, but he told her that Sally was stable after the doctors had given her a tracheostomy. She tried to call Leo, but he didn't pick up; she left a message on his phone asking after Sergeant Henderson.

The grim reminder of the raid's ugly results undid any work the rest might have done towards cooling her temper. The queue at the bakery where she grabbed breakfast made her late, and she arrived at the RCU with a cooling cup of coffee, a bacon sandwich, and a headache.

The detective branch of the Ritual Crime Unit worked out of an open plan office on the second floor. As she pushed through the double doors, heads popped up from behind the computers like startled prairie dogs. No Sally today, of course, but Tim had made it in on time, though he looked dreadful. So much for the resilience of youth. He followed Deepan's cheerful,

"Morning, Guv!" with a vague mumble of his own, sinking back down low behind his monitor.

With the caseload they had, there ought to be more than the four of them, but the budget was tight and not many people stuck it out in the RCU for long. It was an equally bad career choice for both the ambitious and the lazy, dangerous work that rarely came to the sort of tidy conclusion that looked good on a CV.

Deepan crossed the room to greet her as she set her makeshift breakfast down on her desk. "Heard our suspect self-destructed after I left," he said, with an apologetic grimace. "Sorry, Guv. I should have insisted they let me check him over."

She shook her head. "Not your fault. They had Palmer's authorisation to take over—and from what he said, this is coming from over his head. We're officially off the case, kids."

A gloomy silence settled. Sally was usually the one to provide a note of cheer on days when the job was going badly, and without her the office seemed even grimmer.

"Did you get my handcuffs back?" she asked Deepan, to break the silence. The silver cuffs were special issue, and an arse-ache to replace.

"Oh, yeah, Guv." He moved to his desk and opened a drawer. "Got them right here." He held the cuffs out to her by one of the loops. "Good job I remembered. Those blokes were trying to confiscate anything that wasn't nailed down."

"Thieving bastards," Pierce muttered, crumpling her sandwich wrapper to toss at the bin. "*Six months* we've been after this skinbinder." Had Counter Terrorism known where he was operating all along? Or had they been riding along on the RCU's coattails, letting them do all the work before sweeping in to take over?

She spun the handcuffs around her finger as she pondered, the harsh artificial light reflecting off the battered silver.

And also off something else. Pierce raised the cuffs to take a closer look.

A single strand of thick black hair was caught in the hinge. Definitely not hers. She glanced across at Deepan. "Have you been rubbing these cuffs on your head, my son?" she asked him.

"Er... not recently, Guv," he said, giving her a sideways look.

She spun the handcuffs around to show him the strand of hair—or rather, fur. "Then we might still have some evidence from our panther friend after all."

THERE WAS NO point taking the panther hair down to forensics. It would take them weeks to get around to testing it, with their backlog—assuming they would even agree to process it at all, when it hadn't come through proper channels. Besides, she already had a good idea what kind of hair it was and where it had come from.

No, what she needed now was a different kind of analysis. She bagged the strand of hair and took it down to Sympathetic Magic.

Magical analysis was a hodgepodge field, still in its infancy—and utterly useless for securing a conviction. Ritual magic was tough to safely replicate, difficult to record, and harder still to explain to a jury. Sympathetic magic drew the shortest straw of all, since no lawyer on Earth could fail to clear a client charged with harming a victim from miles away with a few fingernails and some hair.

Hence, the station's Sympathetic Magic department was pretty small. About five foot one, in fact, and commonly known by the name of Jenny.

"Jen!" Pierce leaned in through the door of the small office, made still more cramped by stacks of books and file folders. "Got an analysis job for you." She held up the evidence bag.

"Fantastic." Jennifer Hayes peered out at her through a gap between cardboard boxes, a view that showed little more than a glimpse of her silver-framed glasses and wavy black hair. She gestured vaguely towards the left side of the room. "Put it with the other fifty-seven. I'm sure that I'll get caught up sometime in the next few decades."

"This one's a priority," Pierce said, stepping into the room and closing the door behind her. She squeezed her way past a box of ring binders to reach the desk.

"Aren't they all?" she said with a wry purse of her lips, but she shoved a stack of books aside to free up some desk space. "All right. What miracles are you expecting me to work for you this time?"

Pierce set the evidence bag down in front of her. "I need everything you can tell me about this."

She peered at the bag, for a moment more intrigued by the lack of labelling than the dark hair within. "Ooh, unmarked evidence." She looked up with a slight smirk. "What am I doing, hunting down your ex?"

"I don't know when you think I had the time for one of those," she said. If police work ate into your private life, then working for the RCU swallowed it whole and crunched up the bones. They were writing the book as they went along; so much about magic was still undocumented and poorly understood.

"You're telling me field investigation isn't the glamorous rock star lifestyle that I've been dreaming of so long?" Jenny grinned, then bit her lip. "Sorry, I suppose that was poor taste," she said, clearly thinking of the events of the night before. "Any word on how Sally's doing?"

"She's stable." A term that ought to be reassuring, but only served as a dark reminder of how close it had come. "Still waiting to hear from Leo Grey about the Firearms Officer who was hurt."

"Nasty business all round," she said soberly. She studied the hair in its evidence packet. "This is from that?"

"Hair from the shapeshifter's pelt," Pierce told her. "All that we've got left. Some goons claiming to be the 'Counter Terror Action Team' took over our case, seized all the evidence, and managed to give the suspect that we had in custody a chance to off himself while they were at it. Officially, it's no longer our business."

"Officially," Jenny echoed, and gave her a knowing look. She took a deep breath and pushed her chair back to stand. "Well," she said, regarding the unmarked bag. "Obviously, the chain of evidence has been compromised here, so there's no point passing this on to the officers handling the case."

"None at all," she agreed.

"*So*, since it doesn't need to be retained, I could always use it to test a new divination process I've been trying to refine." She slid a sidelong look towards Pierce. "Of course, I'd need somebody from the department to follow up on the results and verify the findings are correct..."

"Well, if it's for the cause of advancing our knowledge of magical forensics..." She spread her hands.

"Absolutely." Jenny led the way down to the ritual lab in the basement.

Unlike the cluttered workstations filling most of the offices, the small square table in the centre of this room stood bare. Etched into the concrete floor around it was a ritual circle, bounded by concentric rings of symbols. On the ceiling above was painted an exact duplicate. Containment circles, there to trap anything that might be raised here; Pierce was careful to stay well outside the bounds.

An industrial refrigerator hummed away to itself in the furthest corner of the room. Beside it stood a row of fireproof cabinets. Jenny fished a key out of her pocket to unlock the leftmost, rooting briefly through shelves of labelled boxes and plastic bags. "Ah, here we go," she said as she retrieved a cloth-wrapped bundle.

She tugged the cloth aside to reveal a crudely made bowl on a metal stand. Oval-shaped and fitted with a metal rim, the polished but uneven surface was the colour of ivory... or bone.

"Is that a skull?" Pierce said, raising her eyebrows.

"Yep." Jenny gave an impish grin as she held it up beside her own head to illustrate the angle at which the skull had been sliced. "Brains not included, I'm afraid, but he does have mystical powers of divination to make up for it. And don't worry—whoever he was, he's a couple of hundred years outside your jurisdiction." She turned the bowl over so Pierce could see the symbols painted inside. "This is a Magnus bowl."

"How does it work?"

Jenny grinned wider as she set the bowl down on the table. "Ah," she said, raising a finger as she moved to the refrigerator. "That's where the goat blood comes in."

"Always reassuring words," Pierce noted as Jenny came back to the table with a beaker of thick red fluid. She set it down next to the bowl, then retrieved a wax candle and a ritual knife from a drawer.

"Right, now, I wasn't kidding about this being an experiment," she said. "We've tried this with hairs from live humans, but where fur from an enchanted shapeshifting pelt fits in, God only knows. *Assuming* that it's viable at all, our best bet is probably divining something that's a common truth for both panther and man. Location of their home, for instance."

"That'd do me."

"Okay. So, I'm going to carve what is *hopefully* the right symbol for home into this candle..."—she made a few precise incisions with the knife—"and then add the magic focus..." She made a deeper slit in the base of the candle and carefully inserted the hair. Then she stood it up in the middle of the skull bowl, and poured blood in around it. "All right," she said, and took a slow, deep breath. "The next step is to light the candle." Her eyes flicked to Pierce. "This might be a good time to mention that if this spell interacts badly with the one on the pelt, it could well blow our heads off."

"Good to know," she said wryly, but made no move to leave.

Jenny fetched a box of matches from the drawer, then shuffled back to arm's-length distance from the table. "Well, here goes." She lit a match and stretched forward to touch it to the candle.

The wick went up as if it had been soaked in lighter fuel. Jenny yelped and scrambled backwards as the candle flame leapt high, burning a dark, vivid red that filled the space with shadows. The wax melted like butter, shrinking rapidly, while the atmosphere inside the closed room grew heavy and greasy. As the sinking flame drew level with the blood filling the bowl, it flashed into a hissing cloud of steam. Pierce flinched back, shielding her eyes from the scalding red mist that boiled outwards.

When she lowered her arm a fraction later, the steam had faded and the candle burned out, leaving behind a nauseating smell like burning flesh. The thick tension that filled the air gradually leaked away.

Beside the table, Jenny rose from her defensive crouch, and let her breath out in a sheepish huff. "Well," she said, half to herself, "let's see what that did."

Moving closer, Pierce saw that the inside of the skull bowl was caked with sticky black clots of dried blood. Random splashes, to her eyes, but Jenny seemed quite satisfied as she hauled over a big book from on top of a cabinet. She paged through the long lists of symbols inside, occasionally pausing to jot one on a notepad.

"Right," she said, after a good deal of rifling back and forth. "Amazingly, I might actually have something for you." She indicated a blood splatter at the centre of the bowl, a crescent moon shape with a cluster of dots. "That's definitely a number—twenty-two, I think. It could be thirty-two." She moved her pen to point at to another misshapen blotch. "And this one I know for sure: that's the symbol for 'path' or 'way.'"

"So it's Twenty-Two Something Way?" That sounded promising.

Jenny raised a hand in a half shrug. "Could be 'Way.' Could be 'Road,' could be 'Street.' It's not an exact translation." She tapped two other clusters of blood spots with her pen. "Which is what makes this part tricky to decipher. So far as I can tell, these are the symbols for 'antlers' and 'wood.' Wood as in planks of, not a forest."

Pierce mulled that over. "Antler-timber." Not the most common street name, she had to admit. What else could antlers stand for? Deer. Stags. Reindeer. Horns. Hornwood? Horntree? She had it. "Hornbeam!" she said aloud. "Twenty-Two Hornbeam Way?"

"You should do cryptic crosswords," Jenny said.

"Ha. I prefer my clues to end with arrests and convictions." She was already heading for the door. "Thanks, Jen," she said.

"I did nothing, I saw nothing, I was never here," Jenny called after her.

CHAPTER FOUR

A LITTLE SLEUTHING turned up the most likely match to the partial address, and Pierce left Deepan in charge of the rest of their caseload while she drove over to check it out.

It proved to be an ordinary residential street, narrow semi-detached houses with small gardens out front. Number Twenty-Two was no different to any of its neighbours, no obvious signs of neglect or suspicious activity to draw attention. There was a car on the drive in front of the garage; bog standard silver Ford, neither new enough nor old enough to be distinctive.

The curtains were closed. Either someone inside didn't want to be seen, or nobody had been home since they'd arrested the shifter.

It was a big house for a single man living alone. Maybe there was an ex? She'd have to ask the neighbours. Considering she was no longer officially on the case, it could be tricky to find an excuse to get inside the house. But there might be someone on the street who'd seen something of use. If the shifter's car was still here, then he must have got a lift, or else he owned a second vehicle. The white van at the barn? Maybe she could get a registration.

Pierce drove on past the house and parked further up the street. No need to betray her interest in the house too soon. One advantage of coming alone was that no one suspected a middle-aged woman in a suit of being police.

It could quickly turn into a disadvantage if someone was lurking behind those curtains. It was a chill October day during normal working hours, and the street appeared entirely deserted. The odds of someone coming to her aid if she called for help were on the anorexic side of slim.

Best not to get in any trouble, then.

She strolled past the front hedge, taking a casual glance up at the windows. Not enough gap round the edges of the curtains to be able to steal a peek. The narrow windows in the door were smoked glass, revealing no more than a useless blur. Pierce pressed the bell, and listened to it buzz faintly inside. No sign of movement.

A second attempt proved just as fruitless. She peered in through the letterbox. There was nothing to see except the foot of the stairs.

Balls. Time to try the neighbours, then.

No one answered the door at the houses to either side, but the old lady opposite proved to be a goldmine—and not just because she offered tea and biscuits.

"Oh, yes, that's Joe and Lisa's house," she said, as she settled down in her armchair with a creak of bones that made Pierce wince in sympathy. "Well, I say Joe and Lisa's. I think Lisa might have moved out, but I could be wrong."

"Oh?" Pierce cocked her head in encouragement as she eyed up a custard cream. There wasn't much need to employ interrogation skills; the woman was clearly delighted to have a chance to chat.

"That's her car, you see, out there on the driveway," she said. "Joe has his own—well, it's more of a van, really, I suppose."

"Do you know the make and registration?" She reached for her notebook, not all that hopeful.

"Oh, I'm sorry, love." The old woman shook her head. "I've never been much of a car person. It's a white van, but that's all that I can tell you." The teaspoon clinked in her cup as she stirred it reflectively. "I think he's a builder or a plumber, something like that—Lisa was always a bit vague. She was the one that I usually spoke to; Joe always kept himself to himself, you know the type."

"But it's been a while since you last saw Lisa?" Pierce pressed her.

"Well, now I come to think of it, it must be a couple of months." The old woman frowned over her cup and saucer. "I asked Joe—I thought she might be ill, you see, or maybe her car was broken down, with it just sitting on the driveway all the time. He told me she'd moved out, but, well, she's done that before, you know." She arched her eyebrows meaningfully. "They were always fighting—not that it's any of my business, of course. I thought she'd be back within the week, but perhaps this time she's thrown him over for good." She took a thoughtful sip of tea and frowned again. "Funny that she wouldn't take her car, though."

"Funny," Pierce agreed with a tight smile.

IT WOULD BE pushing it to claim she believed that lives were in imminent danger, but Pierce thought she'd learned enough to justify poking about. It wasn't impossible to think Lisa could be a prisoner, and if so her captor wouldn't be coming back. She'd be neglecting her duty if she didn't at least take a closer look.

A little investigating proved that the gate at the side of the house was only held closed by a bolt, easily jiggled loose. Pierce rounded the building, warily alert. It *felt* like an empty house, but even in more mundane police work it was a bad idea to trust appearances. Jumping at shadows was a small price to pay to avoid shadows jumping at *you*.

The house's small back garden was more overgrown than the front, but offered nowhere for a criminal to hide. A magpie watched her passing with a suspicious eye, but she was pretty sure shapeshifters couldn't shrink that small. The skinbinder's eagle wings made him a man-sized bird: not exactly inconspicuous in daylight. He'd need somewhere to hole up for the day in human form.

Was this the place?

The house had patio doors, unsurprisingly locked. Pierce looked in on the empty living room. Nothing of note to be seen, except for the fact that the three piece suite had been pushed to the wall as if to clear more floor space. The carpet looked rucked up, and she itched to be inside where she could lift it up to check for evidence, whether criminal or ritual.

No warrant: no such luck. She moved on towards the rear of the attached garage instead. There was a back door, and she halted as she saw that it wasn't completely shut; it had been pushed to, but wasn't quite flush with the edge of the frame.

Just a door swollen by damp that wouldn't close—or was someone still inside?

Her hand went to the malodorant spray fixed to her belt. Wouldn't work so well on humans as on more sensitive noses, but it was still a vile stink that ought to shock anybody enough to give her time to run and call for backup.

She should call for it right now, but she was hesitant to do it, unwilling to blow her cover before she knew that somebody was there.

Exactly the kind of reasoning that got officers killed. Pierce guessed it was good she was old and wise enough to recognise the stupidity of the move—right before she went ahead and did it anyway. She unclipped the spray from her belt, holding it in her pocket ready to whip out. Then she took hold of the doorknob. The door was stiff in the frame, scraping along the ground with a rasp that ruined her efforts at stealth.

Inside, the garage was musty, and dark aside from the light that followed her in through the door. She fished for the penlight that she had attached to her keys, wishing she'd stopped to grab her full-sized police torch from the car. If she hadn't been kicked off the case, she wouldn't need to be sneaking around without proper backup or equipment.

The penlight's narrow beam did little to illuminate the space, only highlighting isolated spots as she flicked it around. Workbenches, tools hanging up on the walls; this garage was clearly never used to store a car. It was crammed with old pieces of furniture and garden tools that filled the space with odd-shaped shadows.

Pierce edged her way in past a rusty, grass-stained lawnmower, moving a folding chair out of her way. The garage smelled faintly of petrol, and under that another, subtler scent that raised her hackles. A rolled tarpaulin lay to one side, and she unfurled the plastic sheet as well as she could in the tight space. Dark streaks and drip stains marred the wrinkled fabric. Oil? She knelt down on the concrete to shine the torch beam closer.

Not oil. Even by the penlight's feeble glow she could see the faint reddish tint to the stains. Blood—but was it human or animal?

A clunk and creak from the front of the garage made her whirl, and she saw the door starting to rise. The sunlight that poured in beneath was blinding, and she squinted to make out the figure silhouetted outside as she fumbled to pull the spray out from her pocket.

Before she could bark out a warning, the man in the doorway spoke. "DCI Pierce." She recognised the cool, calm voice at once. "Perhaps you didn't fully understand my meaning when I told you that your team was off the case."

MAITLAND MIGHT HAVE caught her red-handed, but Pierce was pretty sure he was in no hurry to start disciplinary proceedings. Whatever his mysterious little group were up to, she doubted they could spare the time or stand the added scrutiny.

So she stonewalled to the best of her ability. "I received a tip linking a shapeshifter to this address," she said. Perfectly true, as was the fact she'd promised to protect her source; no need to delve into the details further. "Unauthorised shapeshifting falls under our jurisdiction."

Maitland gave a pleasant smile that didn't touch his eyes. "Of course. Nonetheless, given that you knew my team was working on a similar case in the local area, it might have been wiser to keep us informed."

"It was an unreliable tip," she said. "Might easily have been nothing." She hadn't risen through the ranks to DCI without mastering the art of obfuscating without lies.

"Nonetheless," he repeated, still smiling.

The whole exchange was utter bollocks and both of them knew it, dancing round the subject to avoid complications.

Christ, she hated politics.

She left Hornbeam Way no more enlightened, and considerably more pissed off. Whatever evidence might be found in the dead shifter's home, Maitland and his team wouldn't be sharing.

So what was it about this case that had drawn the attention of Counter Terrorism? She'd yet to see any evidence there was more to it than illegal skinbinding and maybe murder. It rankled to think that she might have to let the case go without even knowing what it had been about.

Pierce stopped at a café to beat her mood into submission with chips. While she was waiting for her food to arrive, she called Deepan on her mobile.

"Nothing new, Guv," he reported. "Just paperwork and cold cases. I let Tim go off to the hospital to visit Sally—he wasn't getting a thing done."

"Sally's doing all right, then?" she asked. At least that was one glimmer of good news.

"Husband said she's doing well." Deepan hesitated. "Sergeant Henderson didn't make it through the night, though. Sorry, Guv."

"Damn." Pierce closed her eyes. She hadn't even had the chance to learn the man's first name.

She felt another sharp stab of resentment towards Maitland. It was her request for Firearms Support that had put the team in harm's way, and now she couldn't even tell them for sure that the sacrifice had been for a good reason.

She took a slow, deep breath. "Okay, thanks, Deepan," she said. "I'll probably drop in to see Sally on my way back, if you're all right holding the fort. No trouble from Palmer about the incident in the cells, I hope?"

"Haven't heard a peep, Guv," he said. "Don't even know if there's going to be an investigation our end—looks like Counter Terrorism are going to handle it internally."

"Brush it under the carpet, more likely," Pierce said with a grimace. "All right," she said, after a moment. "Call me if anything comes up."

The meal could have been five star dining, and it still would have sat poorly in her stomach. She arrived at the hospital to catch Sally's husband picking at a sandwich in the lobby café with the same lack of enthusiasm. He looked exhausted, face papery grey, though he summoned up a wan smile as she crossed the room to greet him. She'd met him before at various work dos, but she still had to dredge for the name.

"Hi, Mike. How's she doing?"

Mike let out a breath as he rose and collected up the debris of his meal, seeming glad to have an excuse to abandon it. "She's doing well, they said. Came out of surgery all right. She was awake for a little bit earlier. Still a bit out of it, though."

"Not surprising."

"She can't talk at the moment, but they've given her a whiteboard," he said, leading the way over to the lifts at the far side. "She wasn't really up to writing anything this morning, but I think she appreciated my artwork."

She smiled and nodded. Oppressive silence fell as they waited for the lift to arrive. As they stepped inside, the doors swished closed behind them, Mike spoke again, abruptly. "Did you catch the bloke?"

It took a moment for her to switch mental gears. "The attacker? Yes. Yes, we did." She wasn't about to mention that he'd died in police custody, or that a second suspect had escaped.

Mike seemed to draw some comfort from it anyway. "That's good to hear." The lift doors opened with a ding and he straightened. "This is it."

He led the way along the antiseptic-smelling corridor, shoes squeaking on the tiles. As they passed through the double doors into the ward, Pierce spotted Sally in the second bed.

She'd looked better. The tracheostomy tube sticking out of her neck was a stark reminder of the severity of her injuries. Wound dressings disappeared below the scoop neck of her hospital gown, and her head lolled back against the pillow. At first Pierce wasn't sure if she was actually awake, but then she turned her head to face them as they approached, managing a fraction of a smile.

"Hello, love," Mike said, dropping a kiss on her cheek. "Feeling a bit better this afternoon?" He turned to Pierce. "I'll just go and get us some chairs."

She couldn't really afford to stay for very long, but it was easier to let him go than try to protest. As he headed back out into the corridor, she turned her attention to Sally.

"You look like hell," she told her. "If you wanted to get out of the post-raid paperwork, there are easier ways." Sally gave another pseudo-smile, clearly a painful effort with her neck in its current state.

As her husband returned with a pair of stacked plastic chairs, she held out a hand towards him and made a flapping motion. "You want the whiteboard?" he guessed. "Hang on. Let me just move the table closer so you can grab it."

He wheeled the small table over to her bedside, and Pierce saw a miniature dry erase board resting on it, with a pen on a string. Sally started to try to sit up to reach for it, with obvious difficulty.

"Whoa, don't strain yourself, love," Mike said. "Give me a second and I'll raise the bed for you."

It took lot of faffing to get the bed raised up and Sally comfortable, but she seemed to have something she was determined to communicate. When Mike uncapped the pen and handed it to her, she scrawled CASE? across the board in shaky letters.

"We caught the shifter," Pierce told her, avoiding more complex explanations. She hoped Sally didn't remember to ask after Henderson. "The other one got away." She didn't want to reveal too much detail in front of Mike, but she couldn't help but press for more information. That glimpse beneath the tarp Sally had taken was the only look at the evidence they'd got. "Did you have something to say about the scene in the barn?" she asked.

Sally started to nod, then winced in pain. Her shoulders were tense and the motions somewhat jerky as she scrawled another word on the whiteboard. This one was considerably less controlled than her previous letters, but the message was still legible.

HUMAN.

Mike smiled fondly and patted her arm. "Believe it or not, love, we already realised that you were only human."

But it was Pierce that Sally locked eyes with, willing her to understand.

A cold ripple slid down her spine as the words clicked together in her head. The last thing Sally had said before the panther had attacked them.

Guv, we've got skins here. But I think they're—
Human?

CHAPTER FIVE

PIERCE DIDN'T LINGER at the hospital for long; Sally was obviously too exhausted to take much more, and her own mind was spinning with the implications of that scribbled word. She couldn't ask for direct confirmation with Mike there, but she was sure she'd understood what Sally meant.

Under the tarpaulin in the barn had been human skins.

They couldn't be shapeshifting skins—at least, not working ones. People had been trying for centuries to bind the enchantments onto human skin, and never had more to show for it than an ugly, bloody mess. The skinbinder they were after must be one more in the long line who'd attempted it and failed.

And yet, if that was true, then why was Maitland after him? There was no reason for the Counter Terror Action Team to take an interest in an RCU case. Not unless it had implications for national security.

Implications like the existence of a ritual that would allow a person to be murdered, skinned, and seamlessly replaced by an impostor. Could it be possible?

She drove on autopilot as she left the hospital, pulling into an empty lay-by when she was a few miles on. This was one conversation she'd rather not have overheard and spread all round the social networks. She pulled out her phone and called a former colleague who'd moved down to RCU Oxford.

"Phil. Got a moment to talk?" she asked when he picked up.

"Well, I'm knee-deep in dismembered bodies right now, but for you I suppose I'd be willing to tear myself away." Phil's broad Yorkshire accent came through just as strong as she remembered, undiluted by his years spent living down south. "Hold on." She heard a few rustles of background noise and then the sound of a door closing before his voice returned, a little clearer now. "What's up?"

"That book you were collecting notes for on human-to-animal transformation. You get anywhere with that?"

"What, in the copious free time I have for writing? No, it's on my list of a million and one things to do when I retire. Why, are you after a reference text? I could probably recommend a few, but nothing you wouldn't have heard of."

"Just wondering if you'd been keeping up with the latest research in the field. Anything new popped up in academic circles about human-form shifting?" New occult texts, whether real or fake, were always guaranteed to spark off a fad for attempts to recreate the rituals.

"That old chestnut?" Phil laughed. "No, nothing new that I've heard—just the same old balls being recycled. Always some idiot convinced they can outdo a thousand years of failures with a ritual knife they bought for twenty quid on eBay."

"Mm. All right, thanks, Phil. Probably just another wannabe with more ego than support for his ideas. Nothing for you to worry about."

But as she hung up the phone, she couldn't help but wonder. In the months they'd been chasing the skinbinder, he'd turned out pelt after pelt that matched the quality of any antique piece that she'd seen. It might just be pure arrogance that led him to believe he could succeed where countless others had failed through the centuries—but what if he was right?

The only way to know for sure was to get a proper look at the skins from last night's raid. Sally hadn't had time for more than a brief glimpse, but closer examination ought to show if they were viable skins or just the remnants of attempts that hadn't worked.

She pressed her lips together. Maitland might have his own forensics team and magical experts, but it would still have taken them a while to process the scene. They wouldn't want to risk damaging the skins by moving them in haste—in fact, why move them at all? The farm was safely isolated and the owners off in Spain, and the skinbinder might well return if they left him the bait. Odds were that Maitland's people hadn't left.

She sent Deepan a deliberately vague text about checking out a lead, and drove back to the farmhouse.

Pierce could tell that she'd hit paydirt when she turned down the farm road. There were unmarked vans still parked there, and when she pulled up beside them, a serious man in a suit hurried over to stop her.

"I'm sorry, this is a crime scene," he said, holding up his hands. "I'm going to have to ask you to get back in your car—"

"RCU consultant," she interrupted, showing her badge and stepping around him without slowing her stride. "I'm here to look at the evidence from the barn—are you cleared to know about this, son?" She gave him a scrutinising look. Nothing cemented credentials quite like challenging other people's.

It put the young guard on the wrong foot, and he faltered, scrambling to keep up with her pace. "Er—Um, I wasn't told—"

"No, I don't suppose you were," Pierce said brusquely, heading straight towards the barn. "Clear it with Jason Maitland—he's the one that called me in. Now, excuse me, son. I have a job to do." She left him hovering uncertainly behind her. Even if he called her bluff and did as she suggested, it would still take time to make contact and find out she was lying. All she needed was a chance to get inside the barn and have a look underneath that tarpaulin.

There were a few people inside, all wearing suits rather than coveralls. Convenient for her chances of blending, but suspicious. They clearly weren't concerned about contaminating evidence; either they already knew the skinbinder's identity, or they were confident that nothing in this barn could help them find out.

The whole setup stank to high heaven. Maitland had to have known that the skinbinder was here before last night, yet he'd kept his people back and let her team shoulder the dirty work. She scowled.

It gave her just the unapproachable aspect she needed to avoid questions as she entered the barn. The space inside was gloomy even with the daylight that poured in through the window at the rear. The dirt floor was still scuffed with the footprints from last night, but the bloodstains only drew her eye because she knew where to look.

She didn't look too long, aware that every moment she gave Maitland's team to think increased her chances of getting kicked out. "So where are these skins?" she barked at the nearest person. "Here?" Without waiting for an answer, she moved to grab the corner of the tarp that she'd seen Sally lift last night.

What lay piled beneath it could have been taken for pigskin at first—until, like an optical illusion, details emerged. A clump of matted dark hair, the curve of a human ear... Pierce gagged and covered her mouth, visceral horror overcoming even her police training. Violent death was nothing new after her decades on the job, but the thought of the callous indifference that it took to peel skin back from flesh and bone and stitch it into a costume for someone else to wear...

She turned her head away, swallowing bile. Her eyes fell on the bloody meat hook where the wolf had hung last night. The half-skinned carcass had been pulled down and covered up with a sheet, but in her mind's eye she saw a human corpse in its place.

She hoped like hell the victims were dead before the skinning began.

She took a slow, deep breath, regaining her composure, and used it as a chance to scan the barn. Her eyes fell on the silver skinning knife below the window, dropped there so the skinbinder could transform and make his flight. He wouldn't have abandoned it by choice; it must have been custom made and difficult to replace. She rose to get a better look at the blade.

Before she'd fully straightened, Maitland's voice spoke from behind her. "Chief Inspector." For the first time he was starting to sound sharp in the place of his previous calm. "At this point, I'm not sure if I admire your persistence or if I should just have you arrested right now."

Pierce swivelled on her heel, refusing to betray her jolt of surprise at his presence. "How about you just give me the answers that I'm looking for?"

"I'm afraid that's not possible. But we should talk." He extended his hand in an invitation that was clearly an order. "This way, please."

As soon as he'd led her out of earshot of the others, Pierce turned to face him. "Human skins. You knew about this?"

Maitland gave a slightly pained looking grimace, the first real expression she'd seen on his carefully composed face. "Perhaps now you appreciate why this is a matter of national security," he said in a low voice.

"They're functional?" she said, still sceptical despite his tone. A collection of convincing-looking skins didn't prove human-form shifters could exist.

"Our information says yes."

Pierce narrowed her eyes. "And where do you get your information? If this is for real, the RCU needs to know about it. This contradicts a lot of things we thought we knew for sure. We can't do our jobs if we're kept out of the loop."

"On the contrary," he said, still keeping his voice down. "It's *vital* that this information be contained. Right now, we don't believe that our target has spread the news, and if he has, it's easily dismissed as empty bragging. But if your department is seen to be reacting to a genuine threat, intelligence agencies and terrorist groups all over the world will take notice. We *must* have the skinbinder under our control before this leaks out."

"'Under control.' As opposed to 'under arrest'?" She shook her head in disgust. "This man is linked to God knows how many assaults and murders—if not by his own hand, then as part of a conspiracy. I doubt these skins come from volunteers who donated their bodies. Did you know that the panther shapeshifter's ex-girlfriend has gone missing?"

"You can conduct an investigation after we've secured the suspect. But evidence of human shapeshifting can't go to trial, and if any of your team saw the skins, they should be informed that they were unviable, failed attempts."

Pierce gave a thin, humourless smile. "You mean you'll trample all over the evidence, and then let us sweep up the loose ends while the real criminal goes free."

Maitland showed off his pearly white teeth in a cold smile of his own. "Not free. I assure you, the skinbinder won't escape us."

"Won't escape incarceration, maybe," she said, holding his gaze. "But what about justice?"

Oh, she didn't doubt that Maitland's team would lock the man away. He'd spend the rest of his life stuck in some top secret facility, earning good behaviour points by putting his skills to work. But what about the victims of his crimes, the people who'd lost friends and family to his blade? They would never learn the truth of what had happened to their loved ones, left to wait in vain for people who were never coming home.

Maitland let out a faint sigh. "Justice is best served by ensuring this man's skills don't fall into the hands of our nation's enemies. As I'm sure you'll realise when you've calmed down from your reaction to last night's events. But I'm afraid that in the meantime I really can't afford to have you interfering in this. Consider yourself placed on leave until further notice."

Pierce held his gaze. "Yes, sir," she said with perfect crispness.

She was pretty sure he understood *exactly* what those words meant, but he just smiled and offered her his arm. "Now, allow me to escort you to your car, just to make sure you don't get lost on the way."

PIERCE DROVE AWAY from the farm—but she didn't head straight home. Even Maitland couldn't object to her using her time off to get a bit of shopping in.

Leeds Occult Market seemed like the perfect place. She drove into the city and found a place to park before taking a stroll through the covered market.

There was always a certain sense of stepping back in time on passing through the stalls to the occult section; leaving behind familiar brands and garish modern logos for strange little stands selling handmade things covered with obscure symbols. A heady mix of scents filled the air: acrid herbs, sweet incense, perfumed oils. She passed stalls stacked with thick leather-bound books, and others loaded with trinkets that claimed to be magic charms.

Most of the goods were cheap knock-offs and silly New Age nonsense: at best just pointless quackery, at worst actively dangerous to use in a real ritual. None of that was the RCU's problem. They had their hands full just dealing with genuine artefacts; Trading Standards could handle the rest.

Occult markets were a con-artist's paradise, but an experienced eye could pick out the real thing from all the junk. Pierce cast a glance over each seller's wares as she passed by, alert for anything illegal even if she was formally off-duty.

A few of the regular stallholders here knew her by name, or at least well enough to share a nod in passing. It was the first place the RCU looked for illegal sales; there weren't many places outside Leeds and London where the occult markets were big enough for criminals to lose themselves in the crowds.

The knife stall was a frequent port of call, for all that its sales were above board. Anyone over eighteen could buy a ritual knife; they were rarely used as weapons outside of your average domestic, since those with premeditated murder on their minds had plenty of cheaper stabbing tools to choose from.

But for ritual preparations, you couldn't use just any old blade. The materials, the shape, the conditions under which it was made, the symbols worked into the blade and handle... all of them made a difference to the kind of enchantments it could be used for. Anyone with half an inkling of what they were doing would have a very specific set of requirements.

And that made knives a very fruitful avenue of enquiry. *If* the seller was willing to cooperate.

"Our Lady Pierce," Harry Draper said wryly as she approached his stall. "Come to harass an innocent businessman again?" He was a big burly bear of a man, the kind that even the most opportunistic thief would think twice about trying to wrestle a knife away from. Six foot and change—lots of change—with a beard you could lose a small pet in, he was close to being literally twice her size.

Pierce wasn't intimidated. In her experience, it was the scrappy little guys with lots of practice taking punches that were the ones you had to watch for in a fight. "It's your guilty customers I'm more concerned about," she said. "I need you to consult your records for me."

He cocked his head, unimpressed. "Got a warrant?"

"Have a heart, Harry," she said, stepping closer as she saw a girl in a green hoodie pause to give them a curious stare. "I've got one officer dead and another badly injured. There was a skinbinder involved, and he left his knife on the scene. Anyone come in today to buy a silver skinning knife?"

"Not that I recall," he said, stonewalling maybe just as a matter of principle. She'd heard that Harry had been in trouble with the police back in his youth, a hazard of being the biggest man still conscious at the scene of a few bar fights. Hard to say if he was covering for a customer right now, or yanking her chain purely for the hell of it.

She pressed on anyway. "Or what about the original knife, do you remember that? A silver skinning knife with a curved blade; would have been sold maybe six months ago to a young man, twenty, twenty-five, with dark hair and rune tattoos on his arms."

"I wouldn't remember that far back," he said. "Old man like me? The memory goes."

He was ten years younger than her if he was a day—but it wasn't Harry's reaction that grabbed her attention. The girl in the green hoodie had jerked at the description, more response than she'd given to the talk of crimes and dead police officers. Pierce swung towards her, scenting a possible lead. "You know someone who looks like that?" she asked.

The girl turned and ran.

CHAPTER SIX

FIRST RULE OF police work: when someone runs away from you, run after them. Second rule: don't be an idiot about it.

The first part was always easier to manage than the second.

Pierce was reaching for her radio to call in for backup when she remembered that she was alone and technically off-duty. *Balls.* She'd better keep up with her suspect.

The crowds that thronged the market worked against her on that front, shoppers still aimlessly drifting or looking around for the source of the commotion. "Police! Stop!" she yelled, which achieved nothing except wasted breath.

If the girl had slowed to a walk and shrugged off the green hoodie, she could have disappeared into the crowd without a trace. Luckily she didn't stop to think but just took off, the clatter of her feet and startled squawks of bystanders betraying her direction. Pierce elbowed her way past gawkers in time to see the girl run through the automatic doors and out onto the street.

She gave chase, though her chest was starting to burn from the effort. Should have had a healthy lunch instead of the most greasy option—and not just today, either. The girl was pulling ahead, youth and fitness on her side, but her boots weren't made for running and the awkward bulk of her shoulder bag was slowing her down.

"Police! Stop!" Pierce yelled again. A lot of bloody good it did. The girl dodged around the bollards at the end of the pedestrian strip and ran out across the road without stopping to look. Pierce winced, anticipating squealing brakes or even worse, but luck carried the girl across the street without disaster.

A big lorry arrived just as she reached the kerb, but she saw the girl veering right, and kept pace with her on her own side of the road. The line of shoppers at the nearby bus stop gawked at them both; Pierce cut across the road in front of their bus as it pulled up.

The pavement on the other side curved round a sharp corner where the road merged into another. The girl ran straight across this road as well, this time earning a blare of horns from a swerving driver and the tail of traffic slamming on their brakes behind him.

On the far side, hoardings closed off a partly demolished building. The girl slung her bag over the top, jammed a foot between the crumbling bricks of the adjacent shop front, and hauled herself up after it. As she stretched up, the sleeve of her baggy hoodie fell back, revealing a ring of runes tattooed around her wrist. Another skinbinder, or at least a wannabe.

"Shit," Pierce said with feeling. Now she had even more reason to copy the gymnastics.

It wasn't pretty. The last time she'd scrambled over a fence had been back in her uniform days, and she'd put on a lot of years and weight around the middle since then. As she dragged herself clumsily over the top, after several false starts, she hoped no one was videoing this from an angle that would show her face.

On the other side of the fence was a patch of rubble-filled waste ground, overlooked by the boarded shell of the abandoned building. The girl hadn't run any further, but stood waiting warily a little further up the slope. Behind her lay a collection of piled wooden boards with symbols chalked and spray-painted all over them. This was clearly a hangout for those who practised the less legal kind of ritual, without the money and resources to keep it behind closed doors.

There was only one thing more dangerous than stupid kids playing with rituals they didn't understand—*smart* kids playing with rituals they *almost* understood. Pierce eyed the girl, wondering which category she fell under.

She was a scrawny kid, somewhere between her upper teens and middle twenties. All sharp angles, not enough meat on her bones for proper curves, with sunken cheeks and hair the grubby blonde of a cheap dye job.

"Who are you?" she asked, watching Pierce with fierce suspicion. "You really police?"

She reached for her badge. "DCI Pierce, Ritual Crime Unit. How about you? You got a name of your own?"

She glanced around the site, wary of having been lured into an ambush, but there weren't many places to hide. Most of the entrances to the derelict building were boarded up, and on the right-hand side a maze of scaffolding would prevent all but the most determined of efforts to squirm through.

"Julie," the girl said tersely, after a lengthy pause spent playing with the drawstrings of her hoodie. Not likely to be her real name, but Pierce had bigger fish to fry than a young would-be skinbinder who might never have done more than talk the talk.

"You recognised that description that I gave to Harry Draper," she said, holding the girl's gaze. "And it meant something, or you wouldn't have tried to run. Who is he?"

It was a worthless description really, nothing more distinctive than the mention of tattoos that almost any skinbinder would have. The fact that Julie had run meant she already had someone in mind, someone who she'd found suspicious even before she'd heard a description matching him.

She gave a defensive shrug. "Look, I don't even know him. He's just some bloke who used to hang around here sometimes. I haven't seen him for months!"

"You know his name?" she pressed.

Another sullen shrug. "Sebastian. That's what he said, anyway. Like I say, I don't know him. Somebody invited him because he had all these books about skinning and stuff, but nobody really liked him. He was a creep."

"He have other friends?" Pierce asked. She tapped her foot when Julie hesitated. "Look, this guy's not your friend, so what do you care? Just tell me what you know, and I'll get out of your hair. I'm not interested in what you and your mates get up to." Not right now, anyway.

"He didn't have friends," Julie said, wrinkling her nose. "But there was this bunch of blokes who turned up at our meetings—dunno who they were, none of us invited them. Craig reckoned they were government and they'd hacked our phones or something, but it was probably just some twat put the meeting up on Facebook." She snorted and shook her head. "Anyway, they showed up, and they were asking all these questions about human transformation—had we tried it, did we know anyone who'd done it and all that shit. They had this book that was supposed to be the ritual for it."

"And what did you tell them?"

"We told them to piss off!" Julie said in a sudden burst of animation. "Human skins? That's psycho stuff. It's all a load of bullshit, anyway. Doesn't work. We figured it was the police trying to fit us up for something dodgy." She glared at Pierce with fresh suspicion.

"But Sebastian was interested in what they were saying?"

And now they were back to the noncommittal shrugs. "I dunno—like I said, he was a creepy bastard. And after those blokes came round, he stopped showing up, so we all reckoned he must have gone off with them. That was about Easter. Haven't seen him since then, so I can't help you, all right?"

Easter: six or seven months ago, roughly the same timeframe in which their skinbinder had become super-active, churning out pelts as if he had a whole menagerie at his disposal. Their efforts to track the source of the animals had got them nowhere; no zoos or wildlife sanctuaries missing anything major, no evidence of an increase in smuggling. Backers with money and connections explained a lot.

That might be why Maitland's team had been holding off before they brought in the skinbinder... but if so, why not keep her department informed and have them call off the raid? It was hard to escape the suspicion there was something shady going on.

Behind them the scaffolding creaked, and Julie whirled to look at it, jittery as a cat. "Look, that's all I know, all right?" she said, tucking her hands up inside the long sleeves of her hoodie. "I don't know who those blokes were, I don't know where they went, and I definitely don't know anything about dead coppers. Can I go now, please?" She tensed, clearly ready to bolt regardless of the answer.

"Who else might know something about Sebastian?" Pierce asked. "You mentioned a Craig...?"

Julie stepped back, shaking her head. "I—"

Another groaning creak sounded from the building behind them. The scaffolding gave an ominous rattle, and Pierce looked up in time to see a dark shadow detach from the edge of the roof. For a moment she thought a chunk of masonry had torn loose—and then her eyes made sense of the falling shape.

Not falling—leaping. "Shit!" She scrambled back towards the fence.

Julie barely had the time to look bewildered before the shapeshifter crashed down beside her in a cloud of brick dust. It was a huge black dog, a mastiff—but no normal dog would have made such a suicidal jump, or bounced up from it unharmed.

It lunged for Julie, and she shrieked, smashing at it with her bag. The dog tore it out of her hands with a toss of its blunt head, scattering the contents across the ground. "Get back, get back!" Pierce yelled at her, but instead she snatched a chunk of broken brick up from the ground to hurl at the shifter. It bounced off like a pebble.

Pierce grabbed for her malodorant spray, but before she

could get close, the dog shifter gave an echoing bark and snapped its teeth at Julie. Her shrieks of fear became a howl of agony as the massive jaws clamped down around her arm.

"Christ!" Pierce fired off the spray, a sulphuric stench that made her gag and her eyes start to stream.

The big dog reeled back, swinging Julie with it, like a toy held in its mouth. She hit the scaffolding with such force that the metal bars jarred loose, and the framework collapsed in on itself in a jangling cascade. The creature dropped Julie's limp body and bounded away, snarling and shaking its head as if to try to dislodge the smell. Chunks of brick and slate roof tiles rained down from the building behind.

Pierce's nausea rose higher as her ears rang from the avalanche, but she swallowed it and ran forward to grab Julie's dropped bag. If she was a skinbinder, she should have the tools of her trade in there.

She cursed as she dug through it, finding only make-up, books and junk. A glance up showed the big dog was turning around to come back, its human mind wresting control back from animal instincts. More discipline than most humans would have shown in a fight—but then, these shifters weren't the usual bored thrill-seekers. She was dealing with people who had killed, and would do it again.

Inside the satchel, her hand closed around a sheathed knife.

The ritual blade that she pulled out was smaller than Sebastian's, lacking the wicked curve and not half as ornately made. But in one important aspect, the two skinning blades were twins—both made of solid silver.

Pierce fumbled to unfasten the leather sheath and release it as the big dog came thundering back towards her. She hadn't trained to fight with knives, only against those wielding them, but all she needed was to do some damage to the pelt.

And not get killed. That would be the real trick.

As the shifter lunged towards her, she kicked the bag its way, but it just flopped over, the undone flap flying up in the dog's face. The moment of obscured vision gave her time to dive away, escaping the snap of its slobbering jaws as she stumbled on a loose brick. Rubble shifted under her feet and she skidded down the slope, swinging the knife in a wide arc as she turned back.

The dog leapt at her, its true size apparent for the first time; the huge frame stretched out longer than she was tall. Pierce lunged forward to meet it, stabbing upward with the blade.

The shifter's own momentum drove it onto the knife, and she felt the shift in pressure as her thrust into solid flesh became a slice through layers of fur and cloth. The body that slammed into hers was a man's wrapped in fur, still heavy enough to knock her off her feet, but with teeth that clicked together harmlessly beside her ear, no longer the dog's mighty crushing jaws. Before he could recover from the jarring shock, Pierce clouted him across the head and shoved him off of her, snatching for the handcuffs from her belt.

"Police!" she shouted. "You're under arrest! Stay down on the ground!"

He ignored her words, or didn't understand them, mind still not caught up to the shift in shape. Instead he staggered backwards, unbalanced on two legs, and tried to bark at her with vocal cords that wouldn't make the sound. The face beneath the mastiff pelt was at odds with the snarl, clean shaven and well groomed like any bland young office worker.

"Stay where you are!" she said again, but it only seemed to snap him out of the haze, his eyes growing more focused as the situation sank in. He turned and ran towards the fence.

"Shit!" Pierce chased after him, but she was too winded to catch up, and he leapt to grab the top of the hoardings and haul himself up. As he swung over, the mastiff pelt flapped away from his back, and she glimpsed the maker's rune tattooed beneath. Just a glimpse—but enough for her to see that it wasn't Sebastian's mark. The pelt had been made by another skinbinder.

What the hell?

For a brief instant she almost contemplated climbing after, but she knew she was too worn out from the previous chase— and that reminded her to think of Julie. She turned to look around for the young skinbinder, and saw her still lying slumped underneath the fallen scaffold.

"Shit," she said again, more heavily, and hurried over. She brushed brick dust off unmoving flesh, and felt for a pulse.

No miracles today. The girl was dead.

CHAPTER SEVEN

PIERCE LEFT THE waste ground over the back fence, with a last apologetic look at Julie where she lay beneath her scaffolding cairn. It stung to flee the crime scene without waiting for the police, but she couldn't afford to get bogged down in the red tape right now—or worse, let Maitland find out she was still on the case. She'd stumbled on something bigger here than one rogue murderous skinbinder, and she wasn't about to let the trail go cold over a jurisdictional pissing contest.

If that was all this was. Counter Terrorism had their own motives for seeking Sebastian, and she couldn't trust their interests were in line with hers. Sebastian clearly had powerful backers, and it was all too easy to believe Maitland would be willing to cut them a deal.

And now it seemed there was a second skinbinder in the mix. The maker's mark she'd glimpsed on the mastiff pelt wasn't used by any of the country's licensed skin shops, and she didn't recognise it as an antique. Of course, that was Sally's field of expertise, not hers. Pierce grimaced. She couldn't drag a woman who was still recovering in hospital into this morass.

In fact, it was better if she kept the whole of her team out of it. Maitland might have been content to just warn her off so far, but he could easily cause trouble if she kept investigating. Pierce was willing to take that risk, but she wasn't about to drag the rest of the RCU down with her.

When she got back to the car, she grabbed her notebook, and sketched the maker's rune as best she could recall it. Part of the design had been obscured, but if she assumed basic symmetry...

As police sirens wailed in the distance, she capped her pen and frowned over the inked scribble she'd produced. A little like an ankh with wings surrounded by a halo; not high art, but at least it was a lead.

Now she just needed someone to decipher it—and luckily, she had someone in mind.

GARY HOLLAND WAS strictly a small time crook, and even that was pushing it. In truth he was mostly just an enthusiastic collector, with a bad habit of getting carried away when it came to purchases that didn't quite square with the law.

He looked distinctly wary as he opened up the door of his small terraced house to let her step inside. "Chief Inspector," he said, with a strained smile. He was an awkward little man, somewhere in his early thirties, with a bald spot and a taste for knitted jumpers that prophesied the old man he'd become. "Now, I don't know what you're looking for this time, but I can assure you, my collection is completely clean. No more Libyan scorpion sting charms for me!"

It was hard not to feel a bit sorry for him. His twitchy mannerisms always made him appear guilty even when he was telling the truth—which he genuinely might be, this time round.

Or maybe not. As she stepped into the house, Pierce was immediately reintroduced to the collection that cluttered every inch of space. If anything, it seemed Gary's hoarding tendencies had grown since last she was here.

Even the narrow hallway was lined with rows of shelves; she had to squeeze her way along. The contents made for a disturbing display: a mangy looking badger paw holding a candle stub; the skeleton of an eel with its eyes replaced by black stones; a taxidermied owl that had seen much better days. If there was a ritual artefact that had once been a live animal, Gary had it, or a framed, authenticated photo of it, or at the very least a set of books and articles about it.

Shapeshifting pelts he didn't have a licence to keep, but that didn't stop him tracking down all there was to know about them.

"You're in luck, Gaz," Pierce told him. "I'm not here to inventory your collection this time." Though no doubt if she did, she would find more than a few things that shouldn't strictly be there. "I'm here for your expertise."

She almost regretted the words when she saw how he puffed up. She suddenly imagined decades of fielding calls from him offering the RCU his expert guidance.

Of course, the way things were going, Pierce might not be part of the Unit long enough for that to be her problem. And besides, right now she needed information, and she couldn't go to anyone that Maitland might be watching.

Gary ushered her through to the living room, as musty and cramped as the rest of the house. There was only one actual armchair, the rest of the space taken up by glass display cases and shelves. He scurried off to fetch a chair from the dining table. "Can I get you something to drink, Chief Inspector?" he asked from the doorway. "Erm, I've only got Diet Coke or soya milk, but..."

Pierce demurred, not least because she didn't want to contemplate what he might serve it up in. As she sat in the armchair, she found herself facing a goat's head with both of its eyes stitched closed. It managed an accusing stare despite the lack of eyeballs. She was pretty sure that if she started asking about import certificates and licences for some of the more dodgy-looking items on display here, their owner would be in a world of trouble.

Best to steer clear of that can of worms right now.

Gary returned to the room with a straight-backed chair, setting it down close enough to hers to make eye contact uncomfortable. "So what can I do for you expertise-wise, Chief Inspector?" he asked with a nervous giggle.

She decided to treat him like the professional he wanted to be. "I need to know more about shapeshifting pelts. I understand you're an expert on maker's marks."

He lit up at the words. "Oh, yes. I've read all the books—*Foston's Guide, European Skinbinders of the Middle Ages, Lost Artefact Pelts of the Ancient Masters...*"

"It's a modern mark I'm looking for," she interrupted. "Could be someone new on the scene. Would you know about that?"

She wasn't sure Gary would have known 'the scene' if it bit him—something it was quite likely to do—but he nodded enthusiastically all the same. "I'm on all the forums"—he remembered who he was talking to—"well, all the *legal* forums, obviously, heh, nothing dodgy." His forehead crinkled and his eyes took on a hunted look.

"Of course," she said, suppressing a sigh. No point hoping that Gary was ever going to learn. She drew the sheet of notepaper from her pocket and unfolded it. "This is the rune. Do you recognise it?"

He took the paper with a confident smile, but after turning it towards him he visibly paled. "Erm, this is a difficult one..." he hedged, and swallowed. "I'm not sure I can help you with this, Chief Inspector." He looked pained.

It could have been just the fact that his claim to expertise had foundered—but that didn't fit the Gary that she knew. He would have prevaricated, *ummed* and *erred* a lot more and come up with creative reasoning to excuse his ignorance. Pierce narrowed her eyes.

"Come on, Gary," she said. "It's not like you to be without a theory. Are you sure you haven't seen it somewhere? Heard somebody mention a new skinbinder on the forums? If anyone would know, it's you." She held his gaze.

Gary tugged uneasily at the collar of his jumper. "Er, well, as I say, it's a bit of an unusual one... No, sorry, never seen it before," he babbled, voice rising to a squeak by the end. He really was a quite appalling liar, but that never seemed to stop him trying it on.

Time to play bad cop. Pierce leaned forward, putting some steel in her glare. "Come on, Gary! I know this is your area. People are hurt!" She opted not to mention that some of them were dead. She didn't know what he might be scared of, but something had him spooked. "Sally Keane's in hospital because of this case!"

"What, Constable Sally?" His eyebrows furrowed in dismay. "Is she all right?" It was Sally they usually sent over to give him a talking to; she had more patience for him than the rest of the department.

"She'll live," Pierce said brusquely. "But it was a close thing, and she's not going to be the only victim if these people aren't stopped." She already wasn't. "If I find out you have information on this and you're keeping it concealed, there could be very nasty consequences."

Gary squirmed for a moment, then collapsed like a heap of blancmange. "You can't tell anyone that I told you," he said in a rush. "They'll come after me. I'll be assassinated. I'll be banned from the forums for life!" It was hard to tell which he considered the more dire fate.

"I'll credit you as an anonymous source," she promised.

He brightened at that, and leaned forward to speak in a conspiratorial whisper. "They're men in black," he said. "Government stooges. That rune is the symbol of a top secret government department. They do all these assassinations, made to look like it's just dog attacks. If you ever see those newspaper articles where people supposedly get killed by their own family pets? It's them."

She should have guessed it would be that kind of conspiracy theorist bollocks. But still, perhaps there was a small grain of truth beneath. Somebody somewhere had once had a reason to connect this rune to a government group.

Like the Counter Terror Action Team, for instance?

Pierce's thoughts were grim as she left Gary's house. It might be just the ravings of a few online conspiracy nutters, but it tied with what her instincts were telling her: Maitland was up to no good. Could he have sent the mastiff shifter to deal with some loose ends who knew too much?

Either way, it seemed clear that he and his team were willing to let innocents die if it helped them achieve their goals. They'd had the opportunity to arrest Sebastian before last night, but instead they'd left him free to keep plying his dark trade until the RCU raid had forced their hand. Had they hoped to study him and learn his secrets before they took the risk of moving in?

Or were they the ones who'd placed him at the farm in the first place?

Her blood was boiling as she drove away. She was sure Maitland was dirty in some way, but what was she supposed to do about it? Take it to the Superintendent? He'd already admitted Maitland's influence extended over his head. Pierce had no personal allies up there where the air was thin, and certainly not anyone who would take her word without proof.

Where and how the hell she could get that, Pierce couldn't begin to imagine.

She was driving without any real destination in mind when she heard her phone ring from the passenger seat. She parked down the nearest side street and picked it up to check the display. Tim. Her stomach flipped. Why would Tim be calling her instead of Deepan?

There could be any number of innocent explanations, but dire thoughts still circled through her mind. Something had happened to Sally. Something had happened to Deepan. Something had happened to *Tim*. "Tim?" she said as she picked up. "What's going on?"

A stomach-clenching pause before he spoke, voice low and hoarse. "DCI Pierce?"

She thought she'd trained him out of being so formal.

"What's wrong? Is Sally all right?"

Another pause. "Er, yeah, she's fine. We're all okay." But he was still speaking barely above a whisper. "But... I need to speak to you. There was a body found in Leeds, a female skinbinder. Chief Inspector... they think you had something to do with it."

Pierce tensed, but she kept her voice level. "Who's 'they'?" she asked, though she had a pretty good idea.

"Um, the Counter Terror Action Team. They took all our files. They said we were compromised. They're listening in on Sergeant Mistry's phone now to see if you make contact, but I managed to sneak off."

"Smart thinking," she said, but inside she couldn't help but wonder. The stilted, careful way that he was speaking, the overly formal terms of address—was it just nervousness at the situation?

Or was someone else listening in on the call?

He might be calling under duress, or simply have been persuaded it was the right thing to do. Tim hadn't been with the Unit long enough for her to expect the kind of loyalty she might from Deepan or Sally. She couldn't blame him for taking orders from people who outranked his superiors.

But if this was a trap, she might be able to spring it to her own advantage. She needed proof beyond doubt Maitland was playing dirty; this might well be her best chance to get it.

All she had to do was make sure that she said all the right lines. "Listen, I had nothing to do with that girl's death," she said. "Someone's trying to fit me up, and I'm pretty sure I know who and why. Are they watching my house as well as the station?"

"They're watching all our homes—but I know where we can meet."

Bingo. Pierce smiled grimly to herself. "Tell me."

There might be an ambush waiting there when she arrived... but it wasn't going to take her unawares.

CHAPTER EIGHT

THE ADDRESS THAT Tim gave her was for an industrial estate, sure to be safely devoid of witnesses after the close of business. It was still just faintly possible the meeting was for real and not a trap, but Pierce wasn't prepared to bet her life on it. After Tim hung up, she considered her options.

Contacting Deepan was out, and the same went for pretty much everybody at the station. There was no way to know who Maitland might be watching. Sally was out of the office, but in no condition to help—if anything, she might well be in danger herself. She'd seen the human skins in the barn, and if that mastiff shifter had been sent to deal with witnesses who knew too much...

She cursed. Sally was a sitting duck at the hospital, and Mike wouldn't be much help. There were a thousand and one ways to arrange for her to suffer a tragic accident, or even a death that looked like natural causes. Pierce wondered now if Henderson had truly died of his wounds, or if someone had taken advantage of his condition to get rid of somebody who'd seen the skinbinder's face. She still hadn't had a chance to speak to Leo.

Maybe she should do that now.

This time she was in luck, and he was there to pick up the phone after only a couple of rings. "Grey."

"Leo, it's Claire Pierce," she said. "Are you free to talk?"

She heard a rustle of papers over the phone. "Yeah, I'm in the office. Go."

First things first. "Sorry to hear your man didn't make it. He was a good officer. Saved all our backsides in there."

A brief pause that she knew was all she would get in the way of a show of emotion. "Appreciate the words," he said, voice as gruff as ever. "Especially since I hear that you've got plenty on your plate. Something going down at your headquarters?"

"Something that stinks to high heaven. Our friend Maitland who took over at the farm might not be what he seems. Turns out that skinbinder we're after has learned some nasty tricks, and Counter Terrorism are willing to do whatever it takes to make sure news doesn't get out. The skinbinder might even be one of theirs."

"Huh," he said, after a brief pause. "Well, that's only the second wildest tale I've heard today, but to be fair, the other one did involve you being wanted for murder."

"I've had a busy day. And it's not over yet. Listen, I need a favour. Can you send someone you trust to keep a watch on Sally? I can't risk showing my face at the hospital again, but it's possible that she could be in danger."

"Where are you going?"

Paranoia held her tongue. She knew Leo would never work with someone willing to sacrifice his people's lives, but that didn't mean that she could trust that his phone wasn't bugged.

"Private meeting. If you need me, ask my team where to start looking." It was as much of a clue as she dared give.

A pretty thin excuse for a safety net, but it beat being wholly alone. She checked the time on her phone after hanging up. Early yet for heading to her meeting with Tim, but if she could scope out the lie of the land before trouble caught up, all the better.

Post-rush hour traffic clogged the roads on her drive back from Leeds, but as she turned off towards the industrial estate she shed most of the company. Isolated cars swished past as she drove down back streets lined with metal fences and near-empty car parks. The buildings were ugly square blocks with small, dim, grubby windows, no sign of anybody still inside. She passed an overgrown, abandoned stretch, strewn with plastic bags and piled with dumped tyres.

It would be an equally good place to dump a body.

Maybe it hadn't been the smartest move in the world to come out here alone, but she was nothing if not stubborn. She took a left onto the industrial estate, passing under a raised barrier and into a cul-de-sac lined with shuttered units. Tim had given her the number of a unit where they could meet; how he'd managed to get access to the place, he hadn't said.

More points towards this being an ambush. But then, she'd still turned up to meet him anyway, so maybe they weren't as stupid as all that.

The potential need to make a quick escape outweighed her desire for stealth, and she parked directly in front of the unit. No sign of Tim's car, but there was a white van parked nearby with a nondescript logo for a company called Solomon Solutions. Could be legit, could be Maitland's people. There was no way to know.

Pierce checked her watch. Six-thirteen—earlier than they'd agreed.

But was she the first one to arrive?

She left the car unlocked when she got out, and kept the keys clutched in her hand. Both the ticket to her quick getaway and a makeshift weapon; she closed her fist around the key fob, leaving the keys sticking out between her fingers. That old classic of self-defence, not much use against someone well-trained and maybe armed, but enough to buy her time to get away.

The door beside the closed shutter had a padlock, but a closer look showed it had been left unlocked. Rather than let herself in, she lifted the letterbox to steal a peek through. It gave a rusty creak, betraying her arrival, and all that she could see was blackness beyond.

"DCI Pierce?" a faint voice said from within. Recognisably Tim, even with the raspy whisper.

Didn't mean it couldn't be an ambush, but hopefully a sign it wouldn't be a fatal one. Two RCU members killed on the same night would draw more attention than she thought Maitland wanted.

Keys still readied, but tucked inside her pocket, Pierce turned the door handle with her left hand. She opened it only halfway, keeping the door between her body and potential attack. "Tim?" she said warily.

"It's just me," he said, though he still spoke in a low voice. He stepped out from the shadows into the dim light spilling in through the door.

He looked terrible, years older than the baby-faced twenty-something she'd left behind at the station just that morning. His face was grey and waxy, and behind the glasses his pale eyes were glazed. Even his hair looked limp, lacking its usual sculpted spikes. Christ, he looked worse than *Sally*, and she'd just had her throat slit.

"Jesus, kid, what did they do to you?" she said, stepping inside.

"I'm all right," he said tonelessly, but she couldn't quite believe it. Not looking like that; not with his face so slack and lacking any of its usual animation. She glanced around, wondering if they were under observation, but the empty unit had been stripped of any fittings that might provide concealment. For now, at least, the two of them were alone.

All the same, Tim moved to close the door, shutting them in together. Pierce shifted her grip on the keys to flick the penlight on instead, the narrow beam providing only just enough illumination to pick out Tim's face.

In the dark, the echoing space abruptly seemed close and confining. A musty smell like something rotting battled it out with the stink of Tim's deodorant. It wasn't like him to take a bath in the stuff; he was clearly nervous about something.

Pierce shone the penlight on him. "Why bring me here?" she asked. "What's so important that you couldn't say it over the phone?" He didn't say a word, just stepped closer. "Tim?" She couldn't read his face, bleached even paler in the harshness of the torchlight. His eyes were blank.

A second later, he was swinging for her head.

No flicker of expression telegraphed the action; the first thing she knew about it was the fist that cracked her across the jaw. She reeled backwards, stunned not just by the impact, but by the source of the attack.

"Tim, what—?" There was no time to gasp the question as a gut punch smashed her breath away. "Jesus—" She barely blocked the next blow with her elbow as she flinched back.

She raised the penlight, trying to get a good look at his face. Completely blank, no sign of murderous rage, panic, or any hint of regret. He was relentless, coming after her in total silence.

It made no sense. Tim wouldn't just *attack* like this, even if he thought she was a killer. He had police training, he was a sweet kid—she would have sworn there wasn't a violent bone in his body.

The fist that flashed towards her head called her a liar. Pierce ducked away from him, retreating, moving further away from the door. It might have been smarter to try to get past him and make a break for her car, but she couldn't leave without finding out why. Was Tim being pressured into this—bribed, threatened, blackmailed? She swallowed the urge to demand he explain himself again. She needed all her breath just to keep dodging.

It was hard to pinpoint Tim in the dark unit. All she heard were soft rustles and her own breathing. She flicked the penlight about, the beam lighting up damp-stained walls, support pillars, the murky shadows.

A faint sound. She spun, just in time to catch him with the beam as he lunged and wrapped his hands around her throat. "Shit!" The word became a wheeze as he dug in with his thumbs. When did Tim get so damn *strong*? Pierce slammed the heel of her hand into his stomach, but it felt like she'd hit a wall of pure muscle. He might look like a gawky kid, but he had reach and youth on her, and she didn't have the strength to force him off.

"This isn't you, Tim," she squeezed out around the crushing pressure.

He gave a guttural laugh. "Oh, you have no *idea*, you stupid old bitch," he said, and now there was nothing in his voice of the Tim she knew at all.

It made it easier to thread the keys between her fingers and slash at his face.

She couldn't miss at this range, with his hands wrapped around her throat, but her strike cut even deeper than she'd aimed. The key's serrated edge tore through his cheek, and he let her go as he reeled back, clutching his face and swearing. The penlight hanging from the keys swung wildly, picking out parts of the room in confusing splashes of light.

Pierce kicked at Tim, but missed him in the darkness, throwing herself off-balance. He shoved her and she went sprawling across the concrete floor, the handcuffs at her belt digging into her side.

Her cuffs. She fought to tug them out as she scrambled back to her feet, belatedly remembering police training. Tim kicked out at her midsection as she fumbled with them, almost knocking her right back to the floor. She wheezed, muscles protesting as she rose and staggered back. She was too old and tired to take much more of this.

She raised the penlight as Tim came towards her. A flap of skin was peeling down from his cheek where she'd slashed it, but in the weak torchlight she couldn't see any blood. A pained rictus distorted his face as he stumbled after her, movements clumsy even though she could swear that she'd barely touched him.

Pierce shone the light straight into his eyes, reflecting off his glasses, and he raised his arm to shield them with a snarl. In the moment he was blinded, she punched out with the cuffs held looped around her fist like knuckle dusters. It jarred her hand, but Tim fell backwards, clutching his nose with a howl.

Before he had any chance to recover from the blow, she lunged forward, snapping the silver cuff tightly around his left wrist.

"Right!" she barked, yanking on the cuffs and shining the light in his eyes. "Enough pissing around! What the *hell* is going on, Tim?"

But the face that she lit up wasn't Tim Cable's at all.

CHAPTER NINE

PIERCE RECOILED IN shock at the sight of her prisoner. Dead skin was peeling away from his face in ragged strips, as if he was about to slough it all off like a snakeskin. Her first thought was another suicide rune, her captive withering before her eyes.

But beneath the peeling outer layer of skin was a whole, unblemished face—a face that wasn't Tim's. A flatter nose, dark-stubbled cheeks, a blunter chin... It was as if Tim's features were a latex mask, pulled on to cover a different face and now disintegrating.

Only it wasn't latex. Not latex at all. Her stomach lurched, and she gagged in horror as she realised what she was seeing.

"*Tim.*" Tears sprang to her eyes, and she turned her head away, half-sure that she would vomit. "Oh, my God, *Tim.*"

Such a sweet kid, an overeager puppy of a constable who hardly seemed old enough to be part of the police force... and now the man who stood before her wore his decomposing remains like some sick parody of a Hallowe'en costume. The real Tim had been murdered, skinned, callously slaughtered just to provide a temporary disguise.

Monsters. Call it skinbinding, shapeshifting, magecraft; however you termed it, the fact remained that she was dealing with monsters.

The shapeshifter made the mistake of taking her grief-stricken shock as a chance to make a break for it. Pierce yanked on her end of the cuffs to pull him up short, not caring how much the metal dug into his skin.

"I wouldn't," she said hoarsely, finding determination despite the sobs catching in her throat. "Enchanted silver. They'll take your hand off before you get out of them—and believe me, I'd be glad to see you try."

"Bollocks," the man said. His voice was nothing like Tim's now, the cruel mimicry of the skin broken by the effect of the silver cuffs. "You're police, you can't do that kind of shit. I've got rights."

"Yeah?" Pierce slammed him back against a pillar. "Bad news, kid. The RCU has a lot more discretion when it comes to magical threats... and in case you didn't hear yet, your friend Maitland just put me on leave. Right now this is strictly personal." She yanked his arms around the pillar and cuffed him there, with his face hugged against the concrete. At least now she could step away and not have to be so close to the evidence of the horror of Tim's death.

"Maitland?" he said, struggling without success to turn his head to face her as she stood behind him. "Who the fuck's that supposed to be?"

"You don't know Maitland? How about Sebastian? That name ring any bells?"

He clammed up, smugly silent, and she was forced to circle round the pillar to see his expression. She shivered with revulsion at the sight of the decomposing skin mask clinging to his face. The features had degraded to the point where she could barely recognise them—a mercy, until she started thinking of the implications. The skin must have been made with extreme haste. Just when had Tim been replaced? Earlier today? Last night? Her gorge rose as she realised that she couldn't even be sure if it was the real Tim she'd seen that morning.

She didn't let her mind linger on it, forced her eyes to look past the peeling skin to the prisoner beneath. If she let herself think of it as part of Tim, she would just lose it.

Playing interrogator was always a type of acting, and right now Pierce needed to sink into the role like never before. She gave her prisoner a cold smile and then moved around the pillar and clasped her hands around the loops of the cuffs. "Oi, what are you doing?" he said, struggling against her grip.

Instead of answering, she gripped the metal tighter, and muttered a low stream of guttural words. The silver already felt warm beneath her touch.

"What the fuck was that?" he demanded as she stepped back. "Hey! What did you just do?"

Pierce didn't answer, walking two slow circuits round the pillar as he squirmed. "Feeling warm yet?" she asked in a conversational tone.

"What did you just *do*, you bitch?" he repeated, metal scraping against concrete as he pulled against the cuffs.

She kept pacing in circles, forcing him to try to twist his neck to follow her. "Just a little enchantment we have on the cuffs for awkward prisoners," she said. "Don't worry, it's harmless—as long as it's stopped in time." She smiled again. "Tell me if it starts to get too hot."

He spat obscenities.

Pierce kept walking, watching as his struggles against the cuffs grew more frantic. "Of course, we don't *really* understand how the spell works," she said. "Magic's funny like that. We know the cuffs will keep on getting hotter until someone deactivates them—but what if they don't?" She gave a theatrical shrug. "No one's ever toughed it out long enough to find out. It could be that the cuffs'll melt, or maybe they'll even get all the way up to cremation temperature... Hell, maybe the spell's got a built-in limit and it'll shut off before you lose your hands." She grinned. "Ready to risk it?"

"Fuck off," he said, but she could see the way that he was fidgeting. Those cuffs had to be pretty warm by now.

Well, naturally. They were silver, after all: guaranteed to cause a reaction with the enchantments on shapeshifting skins. And while a properly made pelt would insulate its wearer from the worst effects of silver burn, she'd seen what happened with the shoddier ones before. This one was disintegrating fast, and whatever protections it might have had to start with, they were failing now. The longer he wore those cuffs, the more the touch of the silver was going to burn.

There was no magical activation phrase to cause it, and it wasn't likely to get much worse than a sunburn or a bite of too-hot pizza—but the power of suggestion was an amazing thing.

"Take your time," Pierce said. "I've got all night. I'm sure that you can take a little pain. Of course, the nerve damage might be a bit tougher to deal with, but—"

"Look, just get these things off of me!"

She dropped the pleasant smile, deadly serious now. "Tell me who you're working for. Tell me where to find the skinbinder who supplied you with that skin. And tell me why you killed Tim Cable!" Her voice broke a little on the last demand.

Her prisoner grinned nastily. "Oh, was that his name?"

She yanked on the handcuffs, pulling him against the pillar with a thump.

"Listen, you moronic little shit," she said, leaning close. "You're dependent on my goodwill not to die a painful death, and let me tell you now, my feelings of love and joy towards all God's creations are not at their highest. You'd better *hope* you've got information worth deactivating those cuffs, because the price tag on that is going to keep rising higher with every moment you dick me around."

He gave a sulky grimace, and Christ, she could have killed him then and there just for that look. Tim had *died* to give this little shit his chance to come after her, but it was clear that he was no fanatic ready to take his own life like the panther shifter—just a petty thug who pouted when things weren't going his way.

A couple more seconds of resentful squirming, and he cracked.

"Look, I didn't kill anybody," he said. "They just gave me the skin and told me to keep you out of the way. I don't *know* why they picked your mate! He was probably just there. They needed somebody police so you would listen to them."

'Probably just there.' Hell of an epitaph for a good man who'd died far too young and in the most horrible way. Had he been alive when the skinbinder had—No. Don't think about it.

"Who's 'they'?" she demanded.

"I don't know, do I?" he said with as much of a jerky shrug as he could manage. "Bunch of blokes from some company doing research into all that ritual shit. I didn't go round asking people's names. A mate of mine got me some work with them before—driving vans, unloading stuff after dark, that kind of shit. I didn't have anything to do with the magic side of it. That was all that freak Sebastian's job."

"The skinbinder." A private company, conducting their own research into binding human skins... then where did Maitland fit in? What about the government dog that had come after her?

"I don't know anything about that kind of shit," he repeated, and rattled the cuffs. "Look, can you get these things off of me?" he whined. "My hands are on fire!"

"Not yet, they're not," she said, without the smallest pang of sympathy. "This company you were working for—what were they called?"

"I don't know!" he said. "Just one of those stupid business-speak names that doesn't mean anything. Sole... solutions? Something like that."

The van she'd seen parked outside. "Solomon Solutions?"

"Yeah, that's it. They've got a place just up the road." He jerked his head. "Look, that's seriously all I know, all right? Now get these fucking cuffs off me before—"

The door rattled. Pierce spun to look, shielding her eyes against the bright beams of the headlights that shone in from outside as it swung open.

She wasn't really surprised to see who stepped in.

"Maitland," she said grimly.

"DCI Pierce." He inclined his head. "Do I trust, now, that you finally believe the two of us are on the same side?"

Pierce still wasn't convinced he was on anyone's side but his own. She stayed silent as a number of men in dark clothes followed him in.

"We'll take custody of the prisoner from here," he said.

"And then what?" she demanded, standing her ground. "He'll just disappear? He's involved in the murder of one of my men!"

"An unfortunate incident that would never have happened if you'd done as you were asked—*ordered*, in fact—and avoided any further involvement in this case."

The cool statement was enough to gut her like a knife, laced with just enough plausibility to keep her up at night. Would Tim still be alive if she hadn't pursued this?

Pierce took a deep breath and then let it out. "Well, I'm involved now," she said. "So I guess it's a little bit late for regrets."

"Quite so," he said, and gave a tight-lipped smile. "You've certainly followed the trail with impressive persistence. But now that we've learned where our targets are based, I'm going to have to ask you to step aside and let my team work." He narrowed his eyes. "In fact, given your track record with following requests, I'm afraid I'm going to have to insist." He turned to address his men. "Remove the prisoner, and have her cuffed in his place. Standard cuffs—keep the silver ones on the shapeshifter."

"Hey, no way!" the shifter blurted, struggling in vain against Maitland's men as they pulled him away from the pillar. "I want these fucking things off me!"

Maitland ignored him, turning back to Pierce. "If you please," he said, inclining his head towards the pillar. She knew the seemingly polite request would soon change tenor if she disobeyed. With a glower, she wrapped her arms around the pillar and allowed herself to be cuffed in place.

"Take her car keys. And her phone," he directed his men. She tensed as brusque, impersonal hands pattered her over, removing the offending items from her pockets.

"You'll be released when the skinbinder is secured," Maitland told her. "Until then, I'm afraid, it's just too much of a risk to let you run free." He dipped his head, though he didn't look the least bit sorry. "My apologies, but you brought this on yourself."

Pierce scowled, but kept her mouth shut; there was nothing she could say that would make him change his mind, and plenty that would get her in worse trouble.

The captive shapeshifter protested as he was hauled towards the door. "Hey, wait, that bitch is the only one who can get these fucking cuffs off! I've got second degree burns here. This is police brutality! I'll sue!"

Maitland turned to her and raised a sceptical eyebrow. "Just how much danger is he in from wearing those?" he asked.

"Might get a skin rash," she said, with as much of a shrug as she could make while handcuffed to the pillar. "Maybe some minor blisters. It's just silver burn—so far as we know, it's completely harmless."

The shapeshifter's furious explosion of swearing as he was dragged away provided a small spot of consolation in what was otherwise a deeply shitty day.

CHAPTER TEN

BEING CUFFED TO a concrete pillar hadn't started out much fun, and it only got less comfortable with time. It was cold inside the unit, and almost pitch black, only the crack of light creeping under the door breaking the illusion of an airtight space. The scent of rot she'd noticed earlier was fainter but still there, and her stomach rolled as she realised it must be the smell of the decaying skin.

Tim's skin. Now that she was alone in the dark with nothing to do except wait, it was impossible to maintain the professional detachment she'd held onto until now.

Christ. Tim, dead. Tim, who they'd teased for being the baby of the office, who'd still carried his spare clothes into work in the battered old backpack that he'd worn to school. Tim, who bought stupid fancy coffee because he didn't like tea—who'd ever heard of a copper who didn't like tea?—and fixed the computers for the rest of the office when the updates clogged the system.

That goofy kid, who hadn't even been born when she first joined the police force, dead and skinned to make some idiot a useless disguise. Pierce tried to rub her eyes with her arm, aware that Maitland's men might come back in at any moment, but in the dark the tears leaked nonetheless.

The minutes ticked past. There was no way to tell how long it had been; she couldn't move her arms round far enough to look at her watch, and the unchanging darkness gave her no clue. She was able to slide the cuffs far enough down the pillar to sit on the floor, but it was far from comfortable, and the cold concrete only made her more aware of all her aches and bruises.

Was anyone still outside, or had they left her here to rot? Only pride stifled the impulse to thump and shout and demand an answer. Maitland had to come back for her sooner or later. If he wanted her dead, he'd have had her killed directly, not left her to a slow death in a place where she could easily be found.

Of course, that assumed he and his men hadn't all been killed by the skinbinder. Pierce counted seconds, making bargains with herself. She could wait a few more minutes before shouting for help. She could wait another couple after that...

An unknown eternity passed before she heard the sound of a car engine approaching. She pushed herself up from the floor, stiff muscles aching in protest. Her heart beat fast. Were they coming to let her out... or to dispose of her now she was no longer needed? In handcuffs, there was nothing she could do to fight back. She took a slow, deep breath, determined not to let her trepidation show.

The door creaked open, and a dazzling torch beam lit the space. She flinched despite herself, her eyes streaming in the sudden brightness. She squinted uselessly, unable to even raise an arm to shield them.

"Claire?" The low whisper of her first name made her jolt in surprise. Not many people used it—she was always 'Guv' to her team, 'DCI Pierce' to most others; only a few longstanding colleagues were on first name terms.

And she recognised that gruff voice even at a muted whisper. "Leo?" she said in disbelief, trying to blink her eyes clear.

"It's me," he said, stepping forward to play the torch beam

over the pillar she was chained to. "Are those your handcuffs?" he asked, raising his eyebrows.

"Do they look like silver to you?" she shot back, before paranoia reminded her he might have good reason to care. She tensed. "Prove that you're really Leo Grey."

"What?" The way that his brow crinkled almost seemed like confirmation; an impostor would know why she was so wary. But that was wishful thinking—she needed proof.

And that bastard Maitland had taken the silver cuffs she could have used to test him.

But maybe that wasn't the only silver around. "Got your silver bullets with you?" she asked.

"I brought my Glock and the rest of the silver-points," he said with a curt nod. "And I'd damn well better get your signature on the paperwork to say you authorised it, because I'm taking your word that the chain of command is compromised."

"Could be far more compromised than I was guessing," she said. God, if they'd got to Tim, who else? "Get one of the bullets out and show it to me."

Leo shook his head, more in bemusement than refusal. "This isn't the best way to convince me that you're not losing it," he warned, but he stepped back and turned away to draw his gun, releasing the magazine with a click. He pushed the topmost round out from the stack, holding it up between his thumb and finger. Even in the half-light, she could recognise the anti-shapeshifter rounds they used, customised hollow-points with cast silver tips. "Satisfied?" he said.

It was only a small amount of silver, but he held it with bare fingers, showing no sign of discomfort. And besides, he sounded a hell of a lot more like Leo than the shifter had been able to impersonate Tim. Pierce let out her breath in a rush and sagged against the pillar.

"All right. I'll believe you're you. Now please just tell me you've got a cuff key with you."

He reholstered the gun and drew his key to let her out. Her arms felt numb and heavy now that they were finally released from the restraints.

"Okay. You want to tell me what that was about?" he asked as she stretched stiffly, massaging her wrists.

"Short version? Shapeshifters in human skins."

Leo frowned. "Thought that was impossible?"

"That's what we thought, but it looks like we're behind the times. I saw it with my own eyes." Despite her best efforts the repressed tears leaked into her voice. "They killed Tim."

It took him a moment. "Your Tim? Cable?"

Pierce nodded, and drew a slow steadying breath. She could fall apart when she got home; right now there was work to do.

"They made a skin of him and used it like a puppet," she said, her fury boiling up as she spoke the obscenity out loud. It gave her a fresh surge of strength and determination after the depression of the dark. "It was falling apart by the time I saw it, but maybe they were just rushed for time. We have to assume they can make skins that allow for a perfect impersonation."

"That's not good," he said, and she barely smothered a painful snort of laughter at the understatement.

"No, it's not. Maitland and his gang went to apprehend the skinbinder, but I don't trust them as far as I can throw them. I don't even know if they've managed to find him. They were supposed to be coming back for me, and that was—" She checked her watch and shook her head, uncertain. "A while back." She focused on Leo, wondering for the first time how he'd even known to look for her here. "How did you find me?"

"You told me I should ask your team," he reminded her. "I called Sympathetic Magic, had them put a trace on you." He cocked his head in response to her look. "That not what you meant?"

"Smarter than what I meant. We might still have a chance to catch up to Maitland, if he hasn't just decided to leave me here for dead. Did you pass a place called Solomon Solutions on your way here?"

A quick search on Leo's phone revealed a suspicious lack of internet presence for any local company by that name. But she'd seen the logo on the van, which was at least proof that some kind of front existed.

The van was gone from outside the unit when they left; most likely it had belonged to the shapeshifter, and Maitland had taken it as a cover.

"Find that van, and we'll find the place we're looking for," she said to Leo. "The shapeshifter said it was close, and I doubt he cared enough to bother lying. We'll just have to scout around until we see it." She eyed the lurid markings of the Armed Response Vehicle that Leo had arrived in and sighed, mourning her confiscated car keys. "On foot," she added wearily. Best not to go flying full police colours until they knew just what they would be facing.

Leo went over to exchange a few words with the officer in the driver's seat of the ARV. Without something immediate to focus on, Pierce felt weariness slump over her like a heavy coat. The day had been far too long, especially coming on the heels of a late night raid.

And it wasn't over yet. As Leo returned from the car, Pierce straightened up, trying to will herself back to alertness. Right now she would have welcomed the North Yorkshire Police's awful coffee—she'd have welcomed dishwater, if it had added caffeine.

"Baker's going to wait here with the car until we call for him," Leo said, though he didn't look all that happy about it. He shook his head. "If Henderson was here, he wouldn't be letting me do this. Nobody in Firearms should be running around playing cowboy without authorisation—and don't tell me I've got yours; it's not worth the paper it's printed on right now."

But Pierce wasn't the only one who'd lost a colleague to this skinbinder and his allies. "If Henderson was here, you wouldn't need to," she said, holding his gaze. "These people are killers, and they *will* kill again. And I don't trust that Maitland cares nearly enough about stopping them from doing it, just as long as he gets what he wants."

He grunted. "That's why I'm coming with you. But I'm not going in shooting without a damn good reason, and if this goes bad, I'm calling for backup."

"Agreed," she said without hesitation.

They started away from the cars and out onto the main street. Pierce stretched her arms, still sore from where she'd been pinned in place around the pillar. She'd kept the cuffs as a replacement for her own: not silver, but still strong enough to restrain a normal human being. Maitland would be a favourite.

"You eaten?" Leo asked her as they walked.

"In one of my past lives, maybe." Her stomach growled.

"Figured. I stole Baker's midnight snacks for you." He offered her a chocolate bar from one of the pockets of his vest.

"Marry me," she said, diving in before she'd even fully opened up the wrapper.

"I think my wife would object," he said, without cracking a smile.

"Well, that's just picky."

The brief boost to her mood from welcome sugar and good humour gave her the energy to keep on walking. The road was deserted, the widely spaced streetlights casting diffuse pools of light that were just enough to give shape to the darkness. A slice of moon showed through the heavy clouds cloaking the sky.

Just past full moon; still a powerful time of the month for lunar rituals. The skinbinder's backers wouldn't want him to miss out on a night's work, and she wasn't sure that Maitland would make too much effort to stop it either. He'd kept a hands-off approach back at the farm, apparently content to watch and learn. Who knew how many murders he might have turned a blind eye to before Pierce had thrown a spanner in the works?

If she had her way, she would throw some more before the night was over.

The businesses they passed were all in darkness, and she had to squint to make out the names on the signs; her penlight was gone with the confiscated car keys, and they didn't want to court too much attention with the bright beam of Leo's police torch. There were fewer vehicles remaining in the private car parks, and she saw no sign of the Solomon van. For all they knew, their quarry was long gone.

"Which way?" Leo asked softly as they reached the end of the road.

Buildings were clustered to their left; more promising than the trees she could see off to the right. She nodded that way. As they rounded the corner, the sound of a car approaching from behind made her tense up. No place to hide; she could only try to move to block the driver's view of Leo in his police gear.

Bright headlights swept over them... and moved on without pausing. Just an innocent passer-by driving down the road. Pierce breathed out.

They followed the rusty fence along. On the opposite side, an access road disappeared around the back of an old yellow brick building. She looked at Leo. "Let's check it out."

The access road lacked street lamps, and the glow of the light behind them diminished as they walked along. Partway down the road metal gates should have barred the way, but despite the late hour they stood open. A security light flashed on as they approached, and Pierce froze in the glare. An angled CCTV camera peered down like a curious robot, but closer inspection showed that it was only the casing, the camera removed from the inside.

Tension coiled in her stomach. This had to be the place.

"Camera thief in this area, apparently," she said. She cocked her head at Leo. "We should probably pop in and check that nobody's in danger, don't you think?"

He grunted in response, his posture shifting subtly into something more alert, more dangerous. He was too much of a pro to draw his gun without good reason, but she sensed the mental switch from a policeman on patrol to a Firearms Officer ready to go in.

She let him take the lead as they continued up the hill. They were hemmed in by a steep bank on the left, a line of metal fencing on the right. It made her think of animals being herded towards slaughter pens. Loose gravel on the rough road surface crunched under their feet.

The light clicked off behind them, plunging them into darkness. She didn't argue as Leo pulled out his torch and switched it on. The element of surprise might have been helpful, but only if it wasn't turned on them. They didn't know who or what might be waiting in ambush.

They crept along the road. No signs of life so far, a fact that only made her nervous. If this was the place, then there should be the chaos of a raid in progress, or else they should have found the scene sealed off against intruders. This dark, stifling silence wasn't right.

The road curved round a corner towards a large brick warehouse. There were vehicles parked up on the verge to the right. Two black vans, and in front of them another with the Solomon logo. Maitland's team?

There were no engines running and no lights on. Had they abandoned the vehicles? She motioned to Leo, and he shone his torch into the window of the nearest.

Empty. They moved on to the next one. Also empty. An odd move to leave their transport unattended. Had the team been overstretched, called the drivers in for back up when they ran into resistance?

Leo went to check the Solomon Solutions van, then paused, shining his torch beam on the back end of the vehicle. "Door's not shut," he said. The windowless white rear doors were a fraction out of flush, the left allowed to fall back into place instead of slammed shut.

Pierce glanced at him. He gave her a nod and drew his pistol, taking up a position to the right of the doors. She stood to the left, out of the line of fire, and rapped on the door. "Police! Identify yourself and come out of the vehicle with your hands up."

No response.

"I am armed and prepared to fire if you make a hostile move," Leo said loudly. "If you cannot speak for some reason, then make a noise to let us know you're in there."

Still nothing. Could be empty—could be trouble. Her chest was tight as she took hold of the door handle. She waited for Leo's acknowledging look, then mouthed a countdown to him. *Three. Two. One...* She yanked the door open and leapt out of the way.

Something dark flopped down from inside of the van. She flinched, anticipating the sharp bark of the Glock, but Leo didn't share her trigger-happy instincts. He let out a slow breath and reholstered the gun as she registered just what had fallen out.

A dangling arm, attached to the body that lay slumped on the floor of the van.

Emphasis on the word 'body.' Judging by the bloody wounds that had made rags of the man's clothes, checking for a pulse would be a waste of time.

Pierce climbed inside the van to do it anyway. The only heartbeat to be found was hers, thumping hard enough in her chest she'd swear it echoed in the closed space. She turned to look at Leo, shaking her head. "Dead." Probably one of Maitland's men. He was dressed all in black, outfitted for a stealth infiltration.

Clearly hadn't been stealthy enough.

Leo reached for the radio on his vest. "Okay, this is the point where we stop doing things off the record," he said. "I'm going to call Baker to bring the car up, and—" He broke off, aware that she'd stopped listening. "Claire?"

Her eyes were on the shadowy shape of the black van behind them; a shape that had suddenly grown deformed as *something* huge and grotesquely misshapen rose from the roof.

"Leo, look out!" she shouted as it sprang.

CHAPTER ELEVEN

LEO BARELY HAD time to turn before the monstrous beast slammed into him. The impact knocked him backwards into the van, and he sprawled across the corpse. Pierce grabbed his ballistic vest to drag him along with her as she retreated towards the van's front seats. The torch clipped to his vest bounced all around, light flickering across the nightmare creature crouched outside.

The pieces the light revealed looked like nothing that should be part of a whole. A bulky, bear-like body, feline paws, vicious curved horns... no creature that had ever walked the Earth had looked like this. Pierce would have sworn out loud if she'd had any breath to do it.

A chimaera pelt. They were the stuff of legend; the one supposed real-life example that she'd seen was a threadbare museum piece most people thought was a hoax. There might be stories of skinbinders with the skill to stitch multiple animal skins into single working pelt, but no reputable source could claim they'd ever seen it done.

Well, if she got out of this alive and with a sliver of her reputation intact, that had changed.

Leo gave a sharp grunt of pain as the thing's claws raked his leg, and she cursed as she hauled him frantically backwards. He wasn't a big man—she doubted he outweighed her—but that didn't make him easier to move. There was no space in the van with the corpse slumped on the floor and the beast swiping at them through the doors like a cat with a cornered mouse.

Her elbow hit the headrest of the passenger seat. "Shit!" She turned to squeeze between the seats. "Leo, come on!" she said. They were sitting ducks inside the van. "We've got to get out of here!" He struggled to rise, and she grabbed his arm to pull him after her.

The whole vehicle lurched, tipping backwards as the chimaera set a paw on the bumper to try and crawl in after them. Its snorting, wheezing breaths filled the inside. Pierce clambered between the seats and dropped into the driver's seat, bashing her knee on the steering wheel as she hauled her legs up after. She cursed as she felt around in the dark for the door release.

Leo's hand groped her shoulder as he fought to keep from falling backwards. There was no chance for him to go for his gun, and firing it inside the metal cage of the vehicle would only put them in more danger. They had to get out of the van.

As the vehicle rocked, Pierce finally managed to grab the handle and throw the door open. Gravity tried to slam it shut in her face, but she shoved her way out and dropped down outside, narrowly escaping being crushed against the fence as the van wheels bounced down after her.

"Leo, come on!" She shoved a hand back through the closing door to help him. He let out a gasping curse as he shouldered his way out, his left leg dragging behind him, maybe clawed up, maybe broken.

There was no time to treat the injury gently. She hauled him with her through the tight space between the vans and the fence. Yet more rusty metal fencing, like the bars at some long-neglected zoo—except the prize exhibit was loose, and they were the ones trapped in the enclosure.

As they ran towards the dark cluster of brick buildings ahead, Pierce stumbled over something soft and yielding. She cursed in startled disgust as she realised that it was another body. Too little light and time to register the cause of death, or even confirm that the man was dead. If any of Maitland's team had survived the chimaera's attack, she was in no position to help them right now.

Just keeping her and Leo alive seemed like a lot to ask. Behind them, the chimaera pulled free of the van with a groan of stressed metal. It gave a strangled, howling roar that didn't sound like any natural creature Pierce had ever heard. Christ knew what kind of jumbled mess of internal organs might exist under that patchwork pelt. It was amazing that the thing was even capable of moving.

And yet it didn't seem to have any trouble persuading its disparate parts to focus on its objective. *Kill.* It scrambled after them at an alarming speed, despite its mismatched limbs.

Beside her, Leo let out ragged gasps with every limping step, but he still fumbled to draw his gun and aim. "Take the torch!" he yelled to her. "I need a clear shot!"

"What, and you think I can help?" At the rate they and the beast were running, she'd be lucky to even find it with the torch beam, let alone hold a steady light on the thing. All the same, she reached for the torch on his vest and struggled to unclip it, turning their already staggering run into a three-legged race. As they reached the corner of the buildings she finally wrenched it free, and turned about to shine it on the beast.

It was barely the length of a lorry away, and crossing the distance fast. In the glow of the torch she glimpsed the thing's eyes, shockingly human amid alien features that blended bear and lion with the curved horns of an ox. The bark of the gun from beside her made her jump. It was followed by a second gunshot, then a third. She flinched, expecting more, but Leo yanked on her arm instead.

"Come on!" he bellowed, the words only half-heard through the ringing echoes in her ears. "Got to get behind cover!"

"Did you get it?" she shouted, and looked back to check for herself. The thing was lurching along now, halfway dragging itself, but it wasn't down, and it hadn't reverted to human. Chimaera skin, shit—it must have more runes, too many layered enchantments for one silver bullet, or even several, to destroy. What would it take to bring it down?

They rounded the edge of the building, hustling as fast as Leo's injured leg would take him. He was stumbling now, relying on the wall and her shoving him from behind to keep him upright as pain began to drown out the panic boost of adrenaline.

Pierce wasn't sure how much more running she could take herself. She was battered, exhausted, and far too old for this. Her breath was rasping in her chest like sandpaper.

She stole another look over her shoulder. Wounded or not, the chimaera still chased. Its back end dragged, no longer fully under its command, but a human mind was still calling the shots; they couldn't rely on it being scared off or convinced to slink away and lick its wounds. It might not be moving too well, but then neither were they, and those jaws and claws and vicious-looking horns could more than compensate if it caught up.

She turned back, and the torch beam swung across a steel door a short distance ahead of her. "Leo!" The door had a security keypad, but it looked as if it had been left ajar. The work of Maitland's people, or maybe left that way in a hasty evacuation.

Deserted or not, the building was their only hope now. She ran ahead of Leo and shoved the door open. Inside, stark fluorescent strip lights lit empty corridors with the institutional look of an old-fashioned school or office.

Not quite empty. A body lay collapsed on the floor in a doorway ahead of them, one slack hand outstretched as if someone had unfurled the fingers to take something from them. Pierce ran forward, crouching over the man to take a pulse, but the glazed eyes and blood-stained mess of his shirt told the story before her fingers could confirm it.

Behind her, Leo leaned against the wall just inside the door, clutching his thigh as he shouted directions into his radio. "Get every Firearms unit in the region that's available. Silverpoint rounds if they've got them. Contact Sergeant Mistry at the RCU—get Oxford RCU on the line as well. We might need them to consult. We have no idea how big this—"

The metal door slammed open, crushing him back against the wall as the chimaera burst in. It was almost too big to make it through the door, the doorframe splintering around it as it forced its way through.

"Leo!" Pierce yelled as she heard him cry out in pain. He sagged to the ground as the heavy door rebounded, falling back against the wall. The chimaera snarled and turned on him, clumsily dragging its back legs behind it. She could see that the bearskin that made up the back half of the pelt was splitting, coming apart where Leo's bullet had taken it in the flank. A bloody mess of flesh and muscle oozed out from between the fraying joins.

The beast was wounded, maybe dying—but not nearly fast enough.

"Leo!" she yelled again, unable to see past the bulk of the thing to tell if he was moving. Was he still conscious? Still alive? She cast around for something, anything, that might work as a weapon, but what could even hurt a shapeshifter that big? She didn't have her silver cuffs or malodorant spray, not even something heavy she could throw. She yanked the corpse beside her closer, searching for a gun or knife.

No weapons. She cursed in desperation.

Pinned in the corner, Leo shifted weakly, trying to rise. The barrier of the door gave him a little protection, but the beast was fishing behind it with its feline front paws. He gasped in pain, and it let out a strangled snorting snarl.

Pierce ran forward, not sure what she could do to help, but determined to try. She lunged to grab the creature's stubby bear's tail, yanking back on it with all her strength. No sound of pain from the beast; this part of the pelt was dead, and it felt like dragging on a heavy fur coat. Stitches tore, the seams never meant to take the strain of joining lifeless fur to animated flesh. Shapeless entrails and tangled, twitching muscles spilled out from the rips, caught in some twisted state halfway between man and beast.

Pierce doubted that she'd hurt it—how would it even recognise a pain signal in that state?—but she'd sure as hell succeeded in getting its attention. The chimaera roared and tried to turn in the tight space, hampered by its unresponsive back legs. She ducked away from the thing's horns; they should look ludicrous on a crossbreed of bear and lion, but the points were too damn lethal to appreciate the joke. Even a sidelong blow could crack her head open.

She was too busy watching the horns to pay attention to the claws. The paw that whipped out to rake her hit with enough force to slap her across the hallway as it sliced her arm open.

"Shit!" She clutched the wound. Not deep, or if it was, the shock was still too fresh to feel it, but the pain was sharp enough to leave her stunned and gasping for breath. She staggered back, leaning against the wall.

No time to rest. Another deadly paw slashed out towards her. She ducked, but not in time to avoid a cuff to the head. Her skull, already ringing with echoes of the gunshots, felt like it was about to break apart. She pressed a hand to her head, struggling to think, unable to plan anything more than a blind retreat. She scrambled back—and tripped over the body in her path.

She caught herself, but her sliced arm buckled beneath her. She hit the ground with a grunt, no breath left for witty last words or even to swear. The chimaera reared over her, its fanged jaws opened wide—

A shot rang out, followed in quick succession by three more. The thing's head jerked backwards, and it toppled like a felled tree. Pierce rolled out of the way just in time as it hit the ground like a sack full of entrails. Inside the loose wrapping of the pelt, the shifter's innards had disintegrated into a shapeless, twisted mass of disconnected organs, meat and bones. There was no way to tell if it was human, animal, or both.

Pierce gave the thing a sharp prod with her shoe as she got up, but it was obvious that it was going nowhere until someone scraped the mess up with a shovel.

That jumble of unidentifiable body parts must have been a human being once. Could the shifter have survived the transformation back if the chimaera pelt hadn't been damaged? No way to know. Messing with untested rituals was never risk free.

Right now she had no pity to spare for the killer who'd worn the chimaera skin. She skirted round the ruins of the corpse and ran across to Leo.

He'd set the gun down on the tiles by his side, the effort of reholstering it obviously too much. His eyes were closed, and his head had fallen back to rest against the bricks. Only his laboured breathing confirmed he was still in there.

Pierce leaned over him uncertainly. "Leo, you all right?" she asked. A bloody stupid question. His slumped position concealed broken bones at least. There was no way that it would be safe to move him.

"Great," he rasped, opening his eyes to narrow slits. "Mind if I... rest here for a while?"

"Long as you're not planning on resting in peace." There were too many people dead already, thanks to this case.

Pierce scrutinised him with concern. She didn't want to leave him, but the building wasn't secured, and there was still a chance the skinbinder was here. "Backup's on its way?" she asked.

Leo made an attempt at a nod that ended with a gasp and grimace. Broken ribs, more than likely. *Fuck.* Not much she could do about it here and now. He licked his lips and took a long, painful pause before he spoke. "Baker's... on his way here," he said with a wheeze, "and I told him to call for..."

"Okay." She cut him off, not wanting to force him through more strained words. "You've got your radio. Just... try to hold it together until help gets here." She patted his arm very lightly, trying not to jar anything that hurt.

He raised his chin as she stood, clearly fighting to say something. He tipped his head towards the pistol by his side. "Still one... silver-point round. You should take it."

She balked, shaking her head. "Leo, I don't have your training," she reminded him. Never mind the regulations—and the *laws*—it would be breaking; they were far enough off the reservation by now that one more rule breach wouldn't make much difference.

Leo shifted his leg as if to push himself further upright before thinking better of it. He focused on her in a squint. "But you've had some?" he said, halfway between statement and question. "Nightstalker Initiative, right?"

"Christ, Leo, that was decades ago!" she said. But he was right; she'd been with the RCU back in the less regulated days when the team still had its own firearms in the office safe. Too many questionable shootings had seen regs tightened up before she'd even been issued a weapon, never mind had to use one in action—thank God—but she'd had the training nonetheless. Such as it was.

Back in those days, wasting expensive ammunition had been a much bigger concern than whether the trainees could hit the broad side of a barn. The old revolver that she'd learned to shoot with didn't much resemble Leo's modern semi-automatic, and her reflexes and eyesight sure as hell weren't the same as they'd been in her twenties. She knew enough not to take her own foot off, but that was about as much as could be said.

Besides, if there was another shifter around, she wasn't the one who was most defenceless right now. "You should keep it," she said.

Leo shook his head, a weak wobble from side to side. "I'm in no state to have a gun in my hand. Just... keep your finger outside the trigger guard unless you want somebody dead." He breathed out in a sigh and held her gaze. "Don't let them get away."

For Henderson's sake, and for Tim's, and for who knew how many other innocents. Pierce took a deep breath of her own and nodded slowly before bending down to take the gun. She hoped to hell she didn't have to use it—but one way or another, she had to bring Sebastian down tonight. Too many people had been hurt to let him walk free from his crimes.

"Stay safe," she said, and turned to go, hoping that this wouldn't be the last time she saw Leo alive.

CHAPTER TWELVE

THE SILENT HALLWAYS of the building were deserted, but signs of the recent struggle were everywhere. Pierce passed three more dead bodies, two of them members of Maitland's team, the third still dressed up in a bullet-riddled wolfskin. Apparently Maitland's people had brought their own supply of silver bullets.

No sound of distant shooting reached her ears; there was no sound at all, beyond the click of her shoes on the floor tiles. If backup was coming, it was still too far away for her to hear the sirens. Without her radio, she couldn't listen out for reassurance, or even check Leo was still alive.

She could have been entirely alone. Maybe she was. But the quiet only wound her nerves still tighter. She checked each doorway as she passed, the gun a deceptively light weight in her hands, almost as threatening as the brooding stillness around her. She had to fight her instincts every time not to let her finger slip towards the trigger, not to point the thing ahead of her with no idea yet what she might be facing.

She should never have agreed to take the thing; she wasn't

trained for it, and she was almost more afraid of putting a hole through an innocent than she was of what might leap out from the shadows. Almost. Her hands sweated on the grip.

The rooms she passed looked like workrooms and labs: books, files and computers everywhere. A field day for the Arcane Documents team, assuming they had the chance to secure the site and seize all this as evidence. Through one door she glimpsed a large storage room, suspicious trophies bagged and tagged and organised on shelves. Pierce itched to get in there and catalogue the artefacts, but now wasn't the time.

As she turned the next corner, the faint murmur caught her ear. Even before she could make out the words, she recognised Maitland's calm voice. She should have known he would have found a way to sidestep the slaughter. But was he her ally or her enemy right now?

That might just depend on who he was talking to.

She crept closer to the voices, straining her ears to pick up the words.

"How far do you think you'll get if you run?" That was Maitland talking, still sounding relaxed. "Your allies have packed up and fled by now, and they won't risk themselves by coming back for you. You've run out of shapeshifters to defend you."

"I can make more." The second voice was low and rough, with an arrogant edge.

"Can you?" Maitland was just as self-assured. "You might have the skills, but you don't have resources. Where do you plan on getting the animals to make pelts? This is England. Missing wolves and tigers draw lots of attention."

"I can do better than wolves and tigers," the other man said, and Pierce's fingers tightened around the gun. This was their man. But what was Maitland playing at? She edged closer to the corner to try and see. The harsh fluorescent lights and bare corridors left few shadows to conceal her movements.

"Maybe," Maitland said matter-of-factly. "But too many missing people will bring even more trouble than wolves. You won't last long without a patron to protect you. Turn yourself in."

"Or what, you're going to make me?" The skinbinder snorted. "You and what army? The one my monsters ripped to pieces?"

Smug youthful bravado, but he had ability to back it up. Pierce stole a cautious look around the corner.

The short corridor beyond led to an emergency exit that must come out at the rear of the building. It had a push bar that would set off an alarm when it was opened, probably the only reason Sebastian had hesitated long enough to cause this standoff. Maybe he wasn't as sure as he'd claimed that Maitland's team were all dead, but so far as she'd seen, he was probably right.

Did Maitland know that?

Right now he was standing a safe distance from the skinbinder, hands slightly raised to signify that he wasn't a threat. Sebastian had his eagle wings strapped to his back again, and he was closer to the door. He could take his chance with the alarm and flee; what was he waiting for?

"I can see you're not the kind to be intimidated by threats," Maitland said. "You're too smart for that—and you're smart enough to realise we can be useful to each other." He held the young man's gaze. "You have abilities we want, and we're prepared to bargain with you for their use. We can help you just as much as you'd help us."

"Oh, yeah?" The skinbinder lifted an eyebrow, the bird wings shifting with his shoulders as he shrugged. "Like how?"

"Amnesty for all your crimes," Maitland said. "A facility—better than this one—with other skinbinders to work as your assistants. The freedom to conduct your experiments without censure or risk of punishment, in return for doing certain jobs for us."

Sebastian cocked his head, smirkingly noncommittal. "That all?"

Maybe he wanted Maitland to offer him more, but Pierce had heard more than enough. She stepped out from the corner, gun in hand.

"How about a counteroffer?" she said. "No bargains, no

amnesty: you're under arrest." She swept her eyes coldly over Maitland, standing unruffled in his immaculate suit, untouched and undisturbed by the life and death struggle that had left at least four of his team dead. "*Both* of you."

She didn't give a damn what kind of authorisation Maitland thought he had. Once he'd started offering amnesty for the darkest kind of murder, he'd lost his right to claim he was on the side of the angels.

Maitland turned towards her with a wry smile. "DCI Pierce," he said, with a faint breath that was almost a sigh. "I should have guessed that you'd turn up sooner or later." He shook his head. "Your resourcefulness does you credit—but I'm afraid you've overstepped your bounds. Even if you've forgotten the fact that you're currently off-duty, you don't have the authority to hold me." His eyes flicked pointedly towards the gun in her hand. "And you definitely don't have authorisation to hold *that*."

"Looking after it for a friend," she said, baring her teeth in a smile. "He decided he was in no state to be in charge of a gun, so he sensibly handed it in to the nearest police officer." She shifted her grip, still pointing the gun at the ground but adjusting her hold as a silent warning. "And I'm pretty sure I have the authority to arrest anyone I believe is breaking the law. Now, both of you—"

The skinbinder made a lunge for the doors, shoving the bar and setting off a head-splitting wail that filled the hallway. Pierce lurched after him with a curse, but her fingers only just grazed the trailing feathers of his wing as he ran out into the night. The ringing in her ears rose to a deafening crescendo as the howl of the alarm sang counterpoint. Maitland shouted something at her, snagging her arm, but Christ only knew what it was he'd said. Pierce shook him off and shouldered the swinging door aside to follow the skinbinder out.

He was running, his head awkwardly hunched forward as he raised his arms—

"Stop right there!" she bellowed after him. "Do not transform, or I will shoot!" She raised the gun, trying to remember how to take up a firing stance. The memories were far too vague for her to be confident of making the shot at anything more than point blank range.

Sebastian paid no attention to her words. Pierce saw his body start to shift, joints stretching and refolding into new, unnatural angles. She should fire—but she hesitated, reluctant to pull the trigger on a suspect who was fleeing rather than fighting. He was a murderer who wouldn't hesitate to kill again, and once he took to the air there would be no way to chase him, but all the same...

"Don't shoot!" Maitland ordered from behind her. "We need him alive!"

It was just the push she needed to remind her of the consequences if the skinbinder escaped to sell his talents to the highest bidder. She held her stance, aimed the gun as best she could. Sebastian was in full eagle form now, fighting to clear the fence...

Don't overthink. Just *shoot*. She squeezed the trigger.

The recoil jerked her hands up and backwards, the bark of the gun so close making her flinch and stumble. Even if she'd had a second bullet, she wouldn't have recovered in time to take the shot. The skinbinder was lost against the shadows of the trees beyond the fence as he dropped from the sky—hit, or just stooping to evade further gunshots? She strained in vain to try and make him out.

Maitland grabbed her shoulder, yanking her further off balance. "If he's dead, I'll see you thrown off the force!" he shouted in her face.

Pierce swung around, throwing her full momentum into a right hook across his jaw. Maitland staggered back, clutching his mouth and spitting muffled swearwords.

There was no time to stop and bask in the satisfaction of the moment. The skinbinder could be getting away.

She ran towards the fence. There were no streetlights back here, and the light of the moon was just about enough to paint the night in shades of charcoal. She should have brought Leo's torch, but she hadn't thought to ask for it while they were still indoors.

She hoped like hell Leo was still all right. If something had gone wrong after she'd left him...

But this wasn't the time to get distracted second-guessing things she couldn't change. Sebastian was out there, and he might not be alone. She couldn't be sure if Maitland's people had properly swept the grounds before they were killed.

If only that idiot had been willing to work with the RCU and the local police, then maybe tonight's bloodbath could have been avoided. But Maitland was playing his own game, and she had to secure the skinbinder and turn him over to the real police before the Counter Terror Action Team could get there first.

The fencing was tipped with lethal spearpoints, too dangerous to climb even if her battered body could have done it. She jogged along the boundary as fast as she could manage, looking for signs of movement in the shadows. On the other side, the hill sloped steeply down to a copse of trees.

Where had Sebastian fallen? Had he fallen at all? She couldn't see a damn thing through the long grass.

She spotted a gate in the fence ahead, and ran towards it at a downhill stagger. As she drew closer, she could see a dirt track, almost concealed by darkness and the grass. The Solomon team must have evacuated this way, and left the gate thrown open when they went. She hadn't heard a vehicle; with any luck, that meant nobody had stayed behind to wait for the skinbinder.

Of course, if he could still fly, that meant exactly nothing. Pierce scanned the cloudy sky for wings as she passed through the gate; a man-sized eagle should be possible to spot even in the darkness. She'd hear the beating of his wings if he took off from nearby.

So where the hell was he?

She left the dirt track to make her way through the long grass, the gun still held in her hand. Empty now, by Leo's count, but she carried it as if it wasn't, a safety precaution and a bluff. Sebastian most likely wouldn't know how limited a stock they had of silver bullets.

Pierce made her way down the hill, alert to every sound. The knee-length grass tangled around her legs, concealing dips and sudden slopes in the steep hillside. Humps of vegetation made false outlines in the dark. She kicked out at a silhouette that looked like a crouching shape, but it was just a hummock in the grass. The cool night breeze had picked up, and the grass bounced and waved around her.

Except in one place a short way ahead, where it stayed flattened to the ground. Her instincts prickled and her footsteps slowed. A wide furrow had been ploughed through the grass here, as if something large and heavy had been dragged down the slope.

Something there, caught in the weeds: a broken feather, far too large for any native bird. Her chest grew tight as she inched closer. Her eyes could now pick out the dark shape slumped on the ground ahead. Sebastian, lying sprawled out on his stomach where he'd fallen, the false wings still outstretched, though one was bent back at an uncomfortable angle.

The silver bullet must have at least clipped him, enough to make him revert back to human. Shit. Her stomach lurched. She'd shot a man with a gun she wasn't authorised to carry, and the fact it had seemed the right thing to do at the time wouldn't help her case much. She couldn't ask Leo to cover for her and claim he'd made the shot himself, and no one would believe he'd been mobile enough to do it anyway.

She approached Sebastian's still form with caution. Was he dead? Unconscious? Just winded? She halted a few feet away. "Don't make any sudden moves," she said, aware she could be giving the warning to a corpse. "I have a pistol full of silver bullets, and I *am* prepared to fire if you make a hostile move. Can you stand up?"

No response. Pierce edged a little closer.

"If you're injured, I will see that you get medical attention. Are you able to speak? If you can make a noise, or move any part of your body, do so now to show me that you're conscious."

She held her breath, but all was silent and still except for the sigh of the wind. She thought she might have heard the distant rise and fall of sirens, but it might just be the ringing in her ears.

Sebastian hadn't so much as twitched. She couldn't tell if he was even breathing. His head had fallen forward in the grass, the curtain of his hair obscuring any clear look at his face. She transferred the useless gun to her left hand as she inched past the wing stretched out in the grass.

Still no movement. Pierce bent forward to check the pale neck for a pulse. As she did, she noticed that the straps that bound the wings to his back had come untied, leaving one of them draped loosely across his shoulder.

A hand shot out from under the wing and grabbed hold of her wrist. As she jerked back, Sebastian reared up, his other hand darting out from underneath his body, holding a knife. She just had time to see the glint of moonlight off the silver blade before it flashed out towards her heart.

She twisted away, but the knife still bit deep into her shoulder. "Fuck!" She stumbled back, the empty gun dropping from her numb fingers as she clutched at the knife hilt jutting out from the wound. How the hell had he carried the knife in eagle form? Some kind of pouch that protected him from the direct touch of the silver? Her mind stuck on the pointless question, her thoughts hazed by the cold shock of a pain she knew she wasn't fully feeling yet. Blood soaked out beneath her fingers.

But she still had a prisoner to secure. As the skinbinder scrambled up, shrugging off the discarded wings like an unwanted blanket, Pierce lunged after him, slamming into his back. He might be younger, faster, more athletic, but she still had the skinny bastard beat on bodyweight.

He went down and she followed him, the hill steep enough to send both of them tumbling. Sebastian hit the rough ground with a sharp cry of pain, and she crashed down on top of him, jarring her wounded shoulder even further.

Her eyes screwed shut in agony, and she didn't see the bony elbow coming as it cracked her across the jaw. Sebastian tried to wriggle away from her, but she caught him by the arm to haul him back. Something in her shoulder felt like it was tearing, and she sobbed with pain, but didn't let him go.

"Get back here, you little bastard," she said through gritted teeth, reaching for the handcuffs on her belt. Not silver, but the standard pair that she'd taken from Maitland would still do for this job. She leaned her weight on him as he struggled and spat and swore.

"You do not... have to say anything," she wheezed, fumbling with the cuffs, "but it may harm your defence"—she snapped the left loop closed around his wrist, strained tears leaking from her eyes—"if you do not mention when questioned.... something which you later rely on in court." He bucked beneath her, almost throwing her off, but she rolled back to pin him down with her knee. "Anything you *do* say..."—with a final gasping grunt of pain, she yanked his other arm into position to snap the second cuff in place—"may be given in evidence," she said, panting for breath. "Understand me?"

He burst into a furious string of swearwords.

"I'm going to... take that as a yes," Pierce said, and slumped down wearily to sit beside him on the hillside. "Now... stay where you are. You're under arrest."

She swallowed as she turned her blurry gaze to the knife hilt still sticking out from her shoulder. The sound of sirens was drawing closer, definitely real this time. All she had to do was stay conscious until backup arrived.

Easier said than done...

CHAPTER THIRTEEN

INJURED AND RUNNING on empty as she was, Pierce had little choice but to turn the skinbinder over to the custody of the local police. She spoke to Deepan, and instructed him to make sure Sebastian turned up where he was sent, no unexpected detours. She also had to break the news about Tim, though she shied away from the full ugly details.

Maitland, it emerged, had disappeared into the night, and taken any of his surviving teammates with him. The police who raided the site found no one else to arrest, just more corpses, some still wearing shapeshifting skins.

Analysing exactly what had happened tonight was going to be a hell of a forensic job, but it was one that Pierce was in no condition to oversee. She was too exhausted and in too much pain to protest being sent away from the scene in an ambulance as soon as she'd spat out the most important explanations. She turned out to be sharing it with Leo, clearly in a bad way even before hospital x-rays could confirm it.

At least he was still alive.

It was hard to celebrate her own survival with enthusiasm once adrenaline and triumph faded. Shoulder surgery, and a long program of rehab to look forward to, plus all the lesser scrapes and bruises she'd picked up along the way. It would be a long, grim and painful recovery, without even the indulgence of self-pity when so many of the people who'd been involved in this mess had come out a whole lot worse.

Few visitors came to see her in hospital. Tim was dead, two good friends were hospitalised themselves, and Deepan was stuck doing everybody's job including hers. The RCU was undersized and overworked as it was, and now it was down by three quarters of its manpower.

So she was surprised when she received a visit from Superintendent Palmer, who she'd always believed to be attached to his desk by an umbilical cord. She was even more surprised that he didn't seem to be there to give her a bollocking.

In fact, he was unusually reluctant to get to the point, avoiding her gaze as he adjusted the front of his uniform shirt. "Ah, Claire," he said, with unaccustomed hesitation. "Shoulder improving?"

"So they tell me," she said. "I'll let you know when the painkillers wear off." At least she was sitting up in the chair instead of lying down; entertaining the boss while still in bed would have been awkward. Pierce really hadn't anticipated a personal visit from him; an elegantly penned Get Well Soon card was really more his style. "Everything all right back at the office?" she asked.

"Er, yes, yes," he said with a nod. "Your... sergeant is doing very well. And there will, erm, be an official investigation into the Counter Terror Action Team's handling of this case. Rest assured that the skinbinder you brought in will be appropriately punished for his crimes." He grimaced, as if aware she wouldn't like what he had to say next. "But it will, of course, have to be handled discreetly. You understand that word of this young man's work can't be allowed to get out."

Perhaps he expected an explosion, and if she'd been healthy

he might well have got one, but right now she was too weary to give both barrels to the debate. Secret courts were nobody's friend in her eyes, but politics was what it was, and those kind of decisions took place far above her head. At least she knew she could trust Palmer to be a straight shooter, far more so than Maitland.

And talking of shooting... there had been curiously little mention of her less-than-legal part in bringing the skinbinder down. Was it all being swept under the rug as part of the general cover-up? The thought didn't sit entirely right with her, but now was hardly the time to go falling on her sword. With Sally in worse shape than she was and Tim dead, the RCU couldn't afford to lose its DCI in charge as well.

Pierce grimaced at her own thoughts. A convenient excuse why 'just this once' the rules had to bend. *That* was a hell of a slippery slope to start down.

Palmer's uncomfortable squirming drew her out of her darkening thoughts. "Well, erm, that's all the news you need to worry about right now," he said. "I should probably get back to the station." He made an abortive move to check his watch, lowering his arm rather awkwardly as a flash of bare wrist was revealed. Things *must* be hectic back at the office if even her immaculately pressed boss was getting ready for work in that much of a hurry.

Or maybe not. Her amusement iced over as she remembered the watch the Superintendent usually worse, the kind of status symbol that immediately marked him out as someone who did his policing from behind a desk. Her own taste in watches ran to the cheap, plastic, and shockproof, but Palmer's favoured wristwatch was far more ostentatious...

And made of sterling silver.

Her eyes snapped up to study his face, but he was already turning to move away. "I look forward to seeing you back at the office," he said over his shoulder.

He looked like Palmer, sounded like him. Her doubts had to be no more wild paranoia.

They had to be... but how could she be sure?

His footsteps faded away into the background hubbub. Pierce shivered in her hospital gown, goose pimples crawling over her skin. She was surrounded by the noise and bustle of the busy ward... but right now, she felt very much alone.

ABOUT THE AUTHOR

E.E. Richardson has been writing books since she was eleven years old, and had her first novel *The Devil's Footsteps* picked up for publication at the age of twenty. Since then she's had seven more young adult horror novels published by Random House and Barrington Stoke. *Under the Skin* is her first story aimed at adults.

She also has a BSc. in Cybernetics and Virtual Worlds, which hasn't been useful for much but does sound impressive.

PAPERBACK—UK: *978-1-78108-095-5* • US: *978-1-78108-096-2* • *£7.99/$9.99*
EBOOK—EPUB: *978-1-84997-542-1* • MOBI: *978-1-84997-543-8* • *£4.99/$5.99*

Five years ago, it all went wrong for Cason Cole. He lost his wife and son, lost *everything*, and was bound into service to a man who chews up human lives and spits them out, a predator who holds nothing dear and respects no law. Now, as the man he both loves and hates lies dying at his feet, the sounds of the explosion still ringing in his ears, Cason is finally free.

The gods and goddesses are real. A tangle of divine hierarchies once kept the world at arm's length, but when one god triumphed, driving all other gods out of Heaven, it was back to the bad old days: cults and sycophants, and the terrible retribution the gods visit on those who spite them. None of which is going to stop Cason from getting back what's his...